"I should have told you about the baby. I should have told you—" She cut herself off.

It wasn't the time to invite her demons into the conversation. Not yet. They'd have to talk about them eventually, but that was a problem for future Maci.

"Why didn't you tell me?" His tone held no malice.

She plopped back onto the couch and looked down at her lap, twisting her fingers over and over. Finally, she decided that if they were going to have a chance at co-parenting—or more—she had to be honest with him. They'd never be able to be anything if she kept hiding the truth. Baby steps.

"I was scared."

"Oh, honey." Just like that, he was kneeling at her feet, big hands cradling her face. "What were you scared of?"

Nothing. Everything.

D0018002

TEXAS BODYGUARD: CHANCE

USA TODAY Bestselling Author

JANIE CROUCH

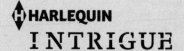

Since this book is about family, it's dedicated to my Kiddo #4. I am delighted to see the woman you're becoming, but you are, and always will be, my baby. Your artistic talent and bullheaded stubbornness amaze me on a constant basis. Go out and do great things in the world!

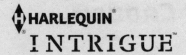

HARLEQUIN®
INTRIGUE™

PLEASE RECYCLE
THIS PRODUCT IS RECYCLABLE

Recycling programs
for this product may
not exist in your area.

ISBN-13: 978-1-335-59112-8

Texas Bodyguard: Chance

Copyright © 2023 by Janie Crouch

For questions and comments about the quality of this book, please contact us at CustomerService@Harlequin.com.

Harlequin Enterprises ULC
22 Adelaide St. West, 41st Floor
Toronto, Ontario M5H 4E3, Canada
www.Harlequin.com

Printed in U.S.A.

Janie Crouch writes passionate romantic suspense for readers who still believe in heroes. After a lifetime on the East Coast—and a six-year stint in Germany—this *USA TODAY* bestselling author has settled into her dream home in Front Range of the Colorado Rockies. She loves engaging in all sorts of adventures (triathlons! two-hundred-mile relay races! mountain treks!), traveling and surviving life with four kids. You can find out more about her at janiecrouch.com.

Books by Janie Crouch

Harlequin Intrigue

San Antonio Security

Texas Bodyguard: Luke
Texas Bodyguard: Brax
Texas Bodyguard: Weston
Texas Bodyguard: Chance

The Risk Series: A Bree and Tanner Thriller

Calculated Risk
Security Risk
Constant Risk
Risk Everything

Omega Sector: Under Siege

Daddy Defender
Protector's Instinct
Cease Fire

Visit the Author Profile page at Harlequin.com.

CAST OF CHARACTERS

Chance Patterson—One of the four boys adopted as a teenager by Clinton and Sheila Patterson. The most strategic. The caretaker. Owns San Antonio Security with his brothers.

Maci Ford—San Antonio Security office manager.

Weston Patterson—The most quiet and serious of the Patterson brothers. Engaged to Kayleigh.

Brax Patterson—The most charming and outgoing of the Patterson brothers. Married to Tessa, father to Walker.

Luke Patterson—Gruffest of the Patterson brothers. Willing to do whatever needs to be done to protect his family. Married to Claire.

Stella LeBlanc—Spoiled social media influencer who has attracted a stalker.

Nicholas LeBlanc—Stella's father and real estate tycoon billionaire.

Dorian Cane—Head of security for Nicholas LeBlanc.

Rich Carlisle—Stella's companion and part-time bodyguard.

Evelyn Ford—Maci's mother, an addict.

Sheila and Clinton Patterson—Adoptive parents of the four Patterson brothers.

Prologue

The moment his alarm rang, despite the fact that the sun wasn't quite cresting the horizon, Chance was up. He didn't have time to waste on snoozing.

He needed to help everyone with breakfast, washing and hair and teeth brushing. Everyone had to be outside for the bus by eight. While the others were eating, he'd check homework and make sure their backpacks were ready to go. Snacks for the younger kids. Change of clothes for the preschool—

"Chance, breakfast is ready!"

Chance froze midway through pulling on his pants and blinked at the darkened room around him.

His room. His alone.

He wasn't in the group home anymore like he'd been for the past four years. There was no small army of other kids around him. No one he needed to help get out the door every morning.

He was at the Pattersons' house. He'd been here for five months now.

He finished getting dressed and walked down the

stairs. He didn't need to make breakfast for a bunch of hungry little kids. Sheila had made breakfast for *him*.

She smiled at him as he walked in the kitchen. "Pancakes. Strawberries on the side for you. The other boys should be up in a minute. Sit and eat."

"Um, thanks." He sat down, still trying to adjust to someone feeding him rather than him being responsible for feeding others. "Do you need help packing lunches or anything?"

Sheila smiled. "Already taken care of. Thank you for asking though."

Right. Already taken care of.

When Sheila shooed him onward, Chance nodded and sat at the six-seater table in the breakfast nook. The room was silent for less than a minute before the others started trickling in.

"Morning, Mom." Brax, Sheila and Clinton's biracial adopted son, kissed Sheila's cheek as he grabbed his plate and sat down next to Chance. "Thanks for breakfast. I'm starving."

"Yes, pancakes!" Luke, their adopted White son came in next, taking his plate and shoving a whole pancake in his mouth before he sat down. Chance winced at the painfully large gulp he took to swallow it, but the others just laughed.

"And that's why I always make yours smaller." Sheila grinned.

The last ones down were Clinton and Weston, who talked quietly on their way into the kitchen. Weston had arrived a few weeks ago, after Chance. The Black boy hardly ever said anything, and worked out in the garden all the time, but Chance liked him.

He liked Clinton too. Sheila's husband was big and Black and funny. He was always respectful to Sheila and didn't yell. He worked as an accountant for some business here in San Antonio.

Sheila joined the rest of the family at the table once they'd all sat down. "Anyone have after-school plans?"

She took a bite of her own pancakes and looked pointedly at Chance's untouched plate. He'd waited for the rest of them too. She didn't say anything, but she didn't have to. With a small grin, he took a bite, knowing it was what she wanted.

What would it be like to have Sheila Patterson as a mom? She was Hispanic like him, so they already looked similar.

Sheila and Clinton had started some of the preliminary paperwork for adopting Chance, but he wasn't holding his breath.

Minds changed. Circumstances changed. Systems changed.

It was why Chance liked to take care of others rather than someone take care of him. That way, if *things changed*, he'd still be okay.

He could take care of himself. He could take care of everyone.

Silence crossed over the table and he looked up, startling when he caught everyone's eyes on him. He'd missed something.

What were they talking about? *Plans.*

"I don't have any plans," he said when the others

kept looking at him. He hadn't realized they'd been asking him.

"Do you want to come hang out with us? We're going to a movie," Luke said, stuffing another pancake in his mouth, only to swallow quickly and painfully again.

Clinton chuckled into his coffee while Sheila pointed at Luke with her fork. "I appreciate that you enjoy my cooking, but you'll eat with some manners at my table."

"Yes, ma'am," Luke said, throwing Chance a wink when she wasn't looking. He laughed under his breath.

"So, movie?" Brax asked.

Chance thought about the cash he'd squirreled away doing odd jobs over the summer. Mowing lawns and whatever side jobs he could get here. He liked having money saved in case he needed it for something.

He did the math in his head. The movie would take a bit of it, but he'd still have plenty left over if he needed to buy new clothes or school supplies once he went back to the group home.

"We're paying for everything, and you could use an afternoon out," Clinton said. "You should go, Chance."

Sheila smiled kindly. "Go be a kid for a change."

Chance wasn't sure he'd ever felt like a kid. There was always too much that needed to be done. Too many people who needed taking care of. Too many bad things to plan for in case they happened.

And in Chance's experience, the bad things always happened.

But he was smart. He knew saying no now would be upsetting to everyone. So he nodded at his foster family. "Okay. A movie sounds good."

The other boys high-fived and started talking about what they would see. Sheila and Clinton smiled at each other.

Chance took another bite of his pancake.

He'd have a good time and enjoy the movie. But despite the happy faces around him, he still knew the truth.

The only one he could rely on was himself.

Chapter One

Abrupt knocking startled Chance Patterson into spilling hot coffee across the back of his hand as he poured it into his mug. He muttered a curse. This wasn't how he'd wanted to start his Monday morning.

The San Antonio Security office—the company Chance had started with his brothers five years ago—didn't open for another hour. He'd come in early in hopes of getting some time to work without interruptions. Obviously, that wasn't going to happen.

Throwing a towel over the puddle on the counter, he pulled out his phone, swiping to look at the doorbell camera.

On the office's stoop stood a man dressed in a suit, carrying a briefcase. Thanks to the HD camera, Chance could see him clearly enough despite the early morning's naturally low light. He had a medium build and was middle-aged and somewhat pale—not unusual for someone who worked in an office full-time.

"May I help you?" Instead of going to greet the man, Chance used the microphone feature on the doorbell.

Security Business 101 was not to open the door to just anyone, regardless of how official they looked.

"Is this one of the Patterson brothers?" The man's voice was clipped and his words concise. Like he was used to only saying what he needed to and not a single word more.

"It is, but we don't open for another hour. If you want to come back then—"

"I can't," he said stiffly, not at all bothered by cutting Chance off or speaking through the microphone. "I'm here as a proxy for someone who wants to hire your services. To whom am I speaking?"

"Chance Patterson. Look, have your employer call us, and we can schedule a time to talk."

"I can't do that either. My employer is busy, and the issue is incredibly time sensitive."

Chance barely refrained from pointing out that he was busy too. He ran his burned hand under some cool water at the sink next to him, while pouring a new mug of coffee with the other. "Who is your employer?"

"I can't provide that information until you've signed a nondisclosure agreement." He waved a manila folder in front of the camera. "His need for privacy is very real, which you will understand if you sign. For now, I can tell you that my name is Benjamin Torres and that your business came highly recommended to my employer by Leo Delacruz. Once you sign the NDA, I can provide further info."

Chance turned the water off and dried his hand. Leo Delacruz was basically extended family at this point. The man had hired San Antonio Security—specifically

Chance's brother Weston—to guard his daughter, Kayleigh, to protect her when a merger got dangerous a few months ago.

Leo was a well-known Texas businessman and associated with a lot of people, so knowing he'd recommended their company didn't narrow down who Benjamin worked for.

The man didn't shuffle or fidget in the silence while Chance thought this through. He came across as not impatient, but efficient. He had things to do and needed his answer.

Chance couldn't give him one under these circumstances. "I'm not comfortable signing something that would require me to keep secrets from my brothers."

The Patterson brothers didn't keep secrets from one another.

Chance grit his teeth. Actually, he'd been keeping a pretty damned big one from them for the past few months.

Benjamin shook his head. "The NDA will permit you to tell your brothers anything you deem necessary, but requires you to keep the identity of my employer and anything he discusses with you confidential, even if you choose not to take the assignment."

"Put the NDA through the mail slot. I'll look it over."

A quick read proved it to be a standard document, with the only changes being what he'd outlined. He could share information with his brothers and their employees as necessary, but no one outside the company. There were no penalties or clauses that would make things difficult if they didn't take the assignment either, so he signed it and unlocked the door, handing the stack of papers back to Benjamin.

"Thank you, Mr. Patterson." The older man tucked the contract into his briefcase and stepped back. "Mr. LeBlanc will be pleased. He's anxious to meet with you all to discuss the situation."

"Nicholas LeBlanc?" The Texas real estate tycoon? He was *big* money. "What exactly does he want to hire San Antonio Security for?"

Someone of LeBlanc's stature would have his own full-time security team.

"Mr. LeBlanc would prefer to give you the details himself. If this afternoon works, he has an availability at 3:00 p.m. Top floor of the VanPoint Tower."

"We'll be there."

With an efficient nod, Benjamin left, getting into the back seat of a town car at the edge of the sidewalk. Chance watched him go, then turned back into the office. He needed to find out as much as he could about Nicholas LeBlanc and get everyone into the office stat.

Looked like a quiet morning working on his own was not in the cards.

"WHY ARE WE all here again?" Luke asked as they stepped into the glass elevator in the VanPoint Tower's lobby later that afternoon.

Chance looked out at the pristine building. "Because Nicholas LeBlanc is the type of client whose recommendation could set us up for years."

Chance and his brothers had started San Antonio Security five years ago. They'd wanted to work together and, between the four of them, had years of prior military and law enforcement experience. At the beginning of their business journey, they'd had to take whatever assignments they could get, which included a lot of following cheating spouses and hunting bail jumpers.

But in the last couple of years, San Antonio Security had grown to become one of the most respected firms in their hometown. Now they did a lot of personal and corporate security—not only the bodyguarding, but situational awareness and tactical defense.

They were brought in by companies and individuals to find and fix the holes in their security, to stop the bad things before they happened.

But sometimes the bad things were already in motion when San Antonio Security was brought in. Chance was afraid that was the case now with Nicholas LeBlanc.

The elevator gave Chance and his brothers a view of the indoor complex that housed a virtual warren of businesses. LeBlanc Holdings held the top two floors—announcing its prestige and prosperity without ever saying a word.

The elevator doors opened, releasing them into a large lobby. People were everywhere, talking, walking, typing. Phones were ringing all over the place, but there was order even in the chaos.

"Mr. Patterson?"

Chance turned and found the man who had showed up at the office this morning. "Yes."

"I was under the impression that you were bringing your brothers with you, not employees. Security downstairs listed you all as Pattersons."

"That's because we are. These are my brothers— Brax, Luke and Weston Patterson."

It was a common misconception, since none of them looked alike.

"I see. My apologies for the error." Once again, Benjamin was all efficiency. "Mr. LeBlanc is waiting for you. Follow me."

Chance followed behind everyone else, taking in the office and the atmosphere. Though the office was guarded downstairs, he saw a man stationed near the elevator and another near the stairs. Both security guards had a line of sight to the door Benjamin was knocking on.

Was it LeBlanc who was in danger then, or was that standard practice?

"Come in." Benjamin pushed the door open, and Chance found himself in a corner office with more windows than walls. The city was sprawled out, with buildings dotting the horizon and tiny people and cars jostling about like ants.

It was the view of someone who had money and power and liked both.

Beyond that, the rest of the room was taken over by a massive desk covered in neat stacks of paper. Everything else in the office, from the carpet to the chairs to the paintings, was done in warm, masculine neutrals. Deep navy and warm gray mixed with the dark mahogany of the bookcases to create a type of space that fit the CEO and founder of a multimillion dollar company.

"Mr. LeBlanc, these are the Patterson brothers, owners of San Antonio Security."

Nicholas LeBlanc stood from behind his desk. "Thank you for coming, gentlemen. Leo Delacruz speaks highly of you. Please sit. Benjamin will get you whatever drinks you want."

Chance took note of the expensive watch and tailored suit jacket. Everything on LeBlanc's body—and in his office—was both extravagant and orderly.

Chance had no problem with either. But once again he was trying to figure out why someone like LeBlanc was interested in a security firm like theirs, even with Leo's recommendation.

Nicholas motioned everyone to a sitting area off to the side of his behemoth desk. They all declined the offer of drinks.

"What can San Antonio Security do for you, Mr. LeBlanc?" Brax asked. As the most charming of the Patterson brothers, he tended to do the initial talking. He had a way of making people feel at ease.

Chance preferred to let Brax talk so he could observe.

"Leo told me that you four were the best at what you do."

"Thank you. We work very hard and pride ourselves on our solid reputation." Brax tipped his head in acknowledgment. "Are you needing more personal security? It seems like you've got plenty."

"Not exactly." Nicholas sighed. "My daughter, Stella, is having an issue. She's a social media influencer, and recently she's become the target of a stalker."

Chance leaned forward, leaning his elbows on his knees. "What kind of stalker?"

"At first it was messages on her social media, comments and DMs from dummy accounts. Then it turned into actual letters being sent to the house with no clue how the individual got the address. Recently it has been bizarre gifts and more. She wants to use what she receives to further build her social media following. Obviously, she doesn't understand the severity of the issue."

"Tell us what you perceive that severity to be," Brax said gently, nodding at Nicholas.

If it was just letters, there wasn't much anyone could do to stop them. Even the police rarely prosecuted stalking cases. There was too much ambiguity to make them stick in court.

Gifts were the same, as long as they didn't cause harm. Icky wasn't illegal.

Nicholas rubbed the back of his neck. "The problem is, no matter what our security measures are, her stalker keeps getting through. We've had Stella on lockdown and they've still gotten letters inside the compound to her. We've gone through three security teams and none of them have been able to stop her from receiving the notes. I'm worried that things are going to get worse, and I don't want my daughter caught in the crosshairs."

Brax sat back, resting an ankle on his knee. "So, you want us to bodyguard Stella?"

Nicholas shrugged. "Yes and no. She has guards on her at all times, though she's not often aware of it. Her constant companion, Rich Carlisle, is someone I hired a few years ago as a social secretary/babysitter. He's also trained in defense, although that's not his primary purpose."

It sounded like Stella had a full team. "Where would we come in?"

"While you might do some guarding and security setup, I'd really like you to focus on finding the stalker. Since we don't have proof of anyone physically harming or threatening Stella, the police can't do anything but write reports. I need someone out there looking for whoever is behind this."

Chance caught his brothers' eyes. They all knew how beneficial this assignment could be for their business overall, but for something like this, everyone needed to be in agreement before they took it on.

Things had changed for his brothers over the past few months. Luke and Brax both had wives now. Brax even had a kid. Weston was engaged to Leo Delacruz's daughter, Kayleigh.

Chance was the only one still alone.

An assignment of this magnitude would take a lot of man hours for everyone, even if Chance took the lead.

It would also mean Chance would be spending a lot more time in the office. A lot more time around Maci Ford, the San Antonio Security office manager.

Who he saw every day, while both of them pretended she hadn't snuck out of his bed in the middle of the night a couple months ago.

All his brothers gave him subtle nods, so he knew

they were okay with taking the LeBlanc assignment. Chance gave his full attention back to Nicholas.

"If we do this, we'll have to split our time between bodyguarding and investigating. It's going to take a lot of planning and strategy."

"I'm willing to pay whatever it takes. You kept Leo's situation quiet, and that's what I need—someone with both discretion and skill."

"This isn't necessarily about the money. What about your own security team?" Brax asked. "Will they feel threatened by us coming in here on top of them? That sort of divided energy makes a difficult situation even harder."

They'd dealt with that exact situation with Leo Delacruz, and it had ended in bloodshed. None of them wanted to take that on again.

Nicholas shook his head. "No, it won't be like that at all. I would not even be here talking to you if my team hadn't vetted you. As a matter of fact…"

Nicholas walked over to his desk and typed something. A few seconds later a man walked through the office door.

He was maybe in his late forties, with salt-and-pepper hair styled neatly to match his black suit. It was tailored, but not designer, and the slightly worn quality of his shoes told Chance he didn't sit behind a desk all day like LeBlanc. He was on his feet a lot.

"This is Dorian Cane, my head of security. Dorian's been with me since I started the company, and he's known Stella her whole life. Dorian, these are the Patterson brothers."

Dorian stepped forward and shook everyone's hand as they introduced themselves. When it was Chance's turn, he watched Dorian's calculating eyes run over him, stopping briefly at the places where Chance had a weapon of some sort stashed. He only missed one, which said Dorian Cane was good at his job.

Chance sat and cleared his throat. "In your opinion, how dangerous is the stalking situation, Dorian? Based on your experience, are these pranks, someone seeking attention or something worse?"

To his credit, the other man thought before he spoke. "It definitely felt like a game at first, but the messages have been getting stranger as time wears on. I'm worried about escalation becoming a very real possibility in the future."

It was one thing for a concerned father to say he thought a stalker was dangerous. It was completely different for someone of Dorian Cane's experience to say the same.

And Nicholas was right. There was nothing about the other man's actions or mannerisms that suggested he felt threatened or angered by their presence.

But Chance asked him anyway. "You're alright with Nicholas bringing us in?"

"My top priority is figuring out who this stalker is. Something about him—although it could be a her—has got all my internal alarms going off. You guys are good. I checked you out myself."

Chance had no doubt that was true.

"I can't let Nicholas's other security concerns fall to the side while concentrating on the stalker. Bringing in people we can trust, who can keep it quiet, is the best solution."

"If we take this job, we'll need to know that Stella will actually listen to us," Weston said. He was the quietest of all the brothers, but he knew from personal experience that trying to guard someone who didn't want to be guarded could be dangerous for everyone. "From what you've said, she may not be interested in that."

Dorian looked over at Nicholas, who gestured for him to go ahead and answer. "Stella is spoiled. She's used to getting what she wants, and she doesn't understand that this stalker isn't something to joke about. It's unsafe and getting more dangerous by the day."

Nicholas adjusted his tie. "Dorian's not wrong. I've definitely spoiled and sheltered her more than I should have, but she's my whole world."

Nicholas reached for one of two framed photos on his desk and held it out to Chance. He took it, nearly doing a double take.

Ah, hell.

"We'll accept the job," Chance said. The picture solidified any doubt he had in his mind.

All three of his brothers looked at him with raised brows until he turned the picture around. Chance wasn't the type to blindly accept any deal without analyzing the details of the contract, but this time was different.

Stella LeBlanc looked exactly like Maci Ford.

And there was no way anyone who had Maci's face was getting stalked on Chance's watch.

Chapter Two

"I've been waiting for this all day."

The soft-spoken words tickled the skin of Maci's rib cage as the feel of warm, calloused hands on her waist made her shiver. She writhed as those hands slid down to her hips, pulling her closer, and those lips climbed to brush her neck and shoulders. She couldn't stop her groan at a soft swipe of a tongue along the hollow of her throat.

"Maci, you taste so good."

Chance's voice was so low it was barely a sound, and the heat of his breath on her skin gave her goose bumps. Threading her fingers through his hair, all Maci wanted to do was feel.

Here in her room there was no work, no clients, no danger. There was only the two of them surrounded by darkness. The pressing weight of him on top of her, the slow glide of their bodies coming together, the touches that anchored them together as they climbed.

Everywhere he touched, her skin burned. It had never been like this with anyone else. She shouldn't have been surprised. There was no one else in the *world like Chance Patterson. Even when he drove her mad, he made her feel more than she ever had before.*

It always made her wonder how hard it would be to survive when he eventually got tired of her, when he realized how bad she was for him.

He nipped his teeth against her collarbone, his palm warm against the side of her throat. "Stay with me, Maci."

He knew her. He may not have known the details of her past, but he knew her need to overthink things that could get the best of her during inopportune moments.

She pressed her lips to his temple. "I'm here. I'm here."

He pressed a kiss over her throat, then continued along the side of her neck, driving her higher until she was gasping for breath. Her nails dug into Chance's back as she found herself falling over the edge. He whispered praises with every sweep of his hips until they were calling each other's names.

As always, there was a moment afterward where they clung to one another. Their breaths mingling, their bodies soft and warm and pliant.

Their hearts unguarded.

It was both too much and never enough for Maci when Chance looked at her then. She had too many secrets to guard, and he was too close to discovering them. Too close to walking away once he did.

Sated and relaxed, Chance pressed a kiss to her head, rolled to the side and tugged her into his arms. Maci tried to pull away, to give them some sort of space so the lines wouldn't blur come morning.

She needed a minute. Just one to rebuild the walls he so easily broke through every time they were to-gether like this. Usually, he let her have some space, but this time he was having none of it.

"Stay with me," he whispered into her hair.

She wanted to. How she wanted to. No matter how short this passion with him lasted, she wanted him with a fierceness that made her feel weak.

Maci Ford was weak for almost nothing, but Chance Patterson was the exception to that hard-won rule. It was as surprising as it was oddly delightful.

When he squeezed her tighter, she smiled and let him drag her close enough that there was no space be-tween them. "I'm not going anywhere."

She didn't want to go anywhere.

She wanted to stay with him.

She rested in his arms and let contentedness wash over her.

But as he fell asleep and the darkness around them became heavier, she knew she couldn't stay. Knew she should've never let this happen again, no matter how much she wanted it. Knew she had to walk away from him—from this.

It was the only way.

Wakefulness came in fits as Maci reached her arm across the bed, expecting Chance's warm skin. At the feel of cold cotton sheets, she frowned and pried her eyes open.

She was alone. Of course she was. She hadn't been with Chance in that way since she'd snuck out of his bed two months ago. She'd made sure he'd known the physical aspect of their relationship couldn't happen again. Even though that had been damn near the hardest thing she'd ever done.

Second only to seeing him every day at the office and trying to pretend like she wasn't interested in him. That they were nothing more than professional colleagues.

She peeked at the alarm clock on the bedside table and groaned. 5:45 a.m. Not enough time to go back to sleep if she wanted to get to the office on time. She spent five minutes glaring at the ceiling—frustrated and wishing that dream had been real—before she tossed the covers off her body. She made her way out of bed and to the kitchen and started the coffee with half-opened eyes.

At least the coffee would give her enough energy to get through the day. Another day with Chance.

Maybe she should get a new job.

She shut down the thought almost immediately. She couldn't do that. Wouldn't. She owed the Patterson brothers for being so good to her. Who else would have hired a twenty-five-year-old with a shiny new GED and no experience?

No one. The Patterson brothers were all upstanding, honorable men. Even before she'd slept with Chance and they were bickering all the time she'd still respected him. She respected all of them. She didn't want to give up her job.

She would have to find a way to continue working for San Antonio Security despite her very nonprofessional feelings for Chance. Which she thought was becoming easier until whatever had happened yesterday when the guys went to meet with Nicholas LeBlanc.

Chance had come back staring at her, even more grumpy with her than usual. No explanation, just a demand that she pull everything she could on the real estate tycoon and his company.

It had been all Maci could do not to tap her heels and salute. She was trying her best not to pick fights with Chance. Jabbing at each other at the office had been fun at first but now had taken a turn for a little more bitter since she'd snuck out of his bed.

She took her shower and got ready for the day, washing the memories of Chance down her drain like she tried to do every morning. Some day she hoped it wouldn't be necessary. But she wasn't holding her breath.

By the time she was ready to go, she was already half a coffee pot into her day and desperately in need of some food before the shakes took over. Still, it was nice pulling into the lot of San Antonio Security as an employee. She loved her job. Loved sorting the guys' paperwork chaos into systems that were tidy and manageable. Loved taking things off their hands and greeting and helping customers.

It was nice to be needed and feel like she was *capable*. That was definitely a first.

She turned off her car and glanced at her cell phone. Swiping away the notifications from her calendar and news apps, she froze. Two missed calls and a text, all from her mother. She stared at the phone, wishing she could toss it out the window.

Delete. She didn't listen to the voice mails. Nothing good came from her mother's mouth before eight in the morning.

Nothing good came from her mother's mouth any time of day.

She glanced at the text from her before deleting it also.

Need to talk to you.

"Of course you do." Maci tossed her phone back into her bag, yanked her keys out of the ignition and opened up her car door.

She fought not to let the text ruin a day that hadn't even started yet. Her relationship with Evelyn had been *strained* for years. Suffering from addiction her whole life, Evelyn treated Maci like a glorified ATM, showing up just long enough to get cash for her next fix before leaving again.

Taking a fortifying breath, Maci got out of her car, holding the handle up—the only way to get the door to stay closed on this vehicle that had seen better years. Evelyn wasn't her problem today.

"Hi, baby girl."

Or…maybe Evelyn *was* her problem today. The sound of her mother's voice was enough to snap Maci's spine straight. Turning quickly, she put her back to the car and stared at the slightly older reflection in front of her.

Evelyn Ford had once been the type of beautiful that people gawked after. Long blond hair that hung in silky waves, icy blue eyes rimmed with thick lashes and an hourglass figure that didn't care what she ate.

Back then, she'd been movie star beautiful. Now, she just looked tired. Almost thirty years of addiction did that to a person. Her hair was still long, but fried and stringy, her eyelashes sparse around dulled eyes. Now her body was thin with scabs from itching. It was like the disease had eaten away at her.

It was everything Maci was terrified of becoming. Everything she'd come way too close to becoming.

It was Evelyn who had sent Maci into such a horrific tailspin that she'd ended things with Chance. A single text threatening to show up had been enough to send Maci packing.

Chance didn't need someone like Maci dragging him down. He had a good family, a job he loved and a great life. There was no room for a high school dropout who'd spent her formative years following in her mother's footsteps. The drugs, the men, the mistakes. Not exactly the type of daughter-in-law Clinton and Sheila Patterson were used to.

No, Chance was better without her and her messy history. No matter how painful it was for Maci.

"You can't be here." Maci leaned against the car door, blocking her mother from view of anyone coming into San Antonio Security. The office wasn't open yet, but the urge to keep this part of her life hidden was stronger than ever. The Pattersons—Chance especially—didn't need to know what Maci came from and who she had to fight not to become.

"You didn't answer my calls." As if it was normal for Maci to be on the phone at 3:00 a.m.

"I was sleeping."

Her mother huffed. "Well, I need your help."

Maci stared at her. If Evelyn wanted help in the form of rehab or counseling, Maci would do whatever was in her power to assist. But that was never the case.

When Evelyn said *help*, she wanted funds to feed her habit, to drown herself in her current drug obsession. "You need money."

Evelyn nodded. She didn't even seem ashamed. Why would she when Maci had been cleaning up her messes since she could hold a broom?

"How much?" It wasn't how Maci would normally handle this but she needed to get Evelyn out of here now before someone saw her and started asking questions. That was the problem with working for a bunch of highly-trained security guys.

Her mother shifted on her feet, now looking sheepish. It was an act, one Maci was all too familiar with. Gritting her teeth, Maci wished she could just walk away from Evelyn. But she would follow. Telling her she shouldn't be here would just ensure she showed up again.

"Three hundred."

Maci sighed but was once again grateful she'd gotten her life together. Three hundred dollars was a lot, but Maci had made sure she had money in savings and enough in her checking to cover three months of bills if she needed.

There had been way too long when she had absolutely nothing.

"How's Pop?"

Evelyn waved one bony hand. "Same old, same old."

Hugo Ford's drug of choice was alcohol. The last time Maci had seen him had been the week after she turned eighteen. He'd thrown her out of the house in a booze-filled rage, and she'd never returned. Still, she'd never been able to put him out of her mind. It was exhausting constantly worrying about people who didn't care about themselves or her.

The rumbling sound of a familiar engine pushed Maci into action. She thrust her hand into her purse and pulled out her wallet, quickly counting out as much cash as she had. Maci held out the stack of bills, but didn't let go when Evelyn grabbed it. "This is all I have, Mom. You're wiping me out."

"Yeah, yeah. I know. This is the last time."

Maci didn't believe that even for a second. She let go of the money as Evelyn nodded then tucked the bills in her pocket and her hair behind her ear. Then without a word she was gone.

No hug, no thanks. It should hurt, but all Maci felt was relief that she was gone.

"Who was that?"

Everything in her body responded to the deep timbre of Chance Patterson's voice. She'd been helpless against it from the very first day.

She spun, just as affected by his appearance. All long legs and broad shoulders, as if he could easily carry the weight of the world—and Maci knew for a fact he tried regularly to do. His face was too rough to be traditionally handsome—jaw and cheekbones hard and unforgiving.

The only thing soft about him were his eyes. Brown, but not a traditional brown—a lighter color, more of a molten honey.

She knew full well how those eyes could pin someone. Make them feel like they were the only person in the world when Chance's attention was on them.

"Who was that?" he asked again.

"Good morning to you too," she said, straightening her purse strap on her shoulder. There was no way she was going to explain the situation with her mother to him.

Those honey eyes narrowed. "Was that lady bothering you?"

She shook her head and started walking toward the office door. "No. Just wanted to know where she could buy tampons."

Chance had three brothers and no sisters. Maci was betting on the fact that the word *tampon* would shut him up.

It worked. He let it go, walking with her toward the office.

"The Nicholas LeBlanc case might get messy," Chance said. "Let one of us know if anything is happening out of the norm."

She had no idea why he would think the LeBlanc case would affect her, but she nodded. She didn't want to start the morning with a fight.

Chance unlocked the door and held it open for her.

She walked through, heading toward her desk in the lobby.

"Maci," he said and she stopped, turning to him.

Those eyes pinned her for a long moment. She wanted to be unaffected but knew that was the opposite from the truth.

"Yes?" she finally asked when he didn't say anything else.

He still kept looking at her.

I've been waiting for this all day.

This morning's dream came crashing back into her mind, as well as the heat that went along with it.

They were alone here in the office. Chance was always early. Nobody else would be here for at least another forty-five minutes.

She took a step toward him as if she was being pulled by a string.

"Chance?" she whispered.

He took a step toward her also.

She shouldn't do this—shouldn't let the moment build between them. But she was powerless to stop it. Powerless to resist those eyes. That jaw. Those cheekbones.

The man.

They both took another step, but then Chance blinked and stopped. He stiffened, backing away from her.

The moment was lost.

"Good morning," he said. Then without another word, he turned and walked to his office, closing the door behind him.

Chapter Three

In all her time of working for them, Maci had never seen the Patterson brothers as flustered as they were working the LeBlanc case.

After their meeting with Nicholas LeBlanc, they'd camped out at the conference room table with the case notes from the tycoon's head of security. Dorian Cane and his team had collected all the stalker's letters and gifts as evidence, storing them carefully since LeBlanc hadn't wanted to bring in law enforcement. That meant one wall of the San Antonio Security conference room was now piled high with boxes of letters, notes and printed photographs, plus the reports to go along with everything.

Three days and too many pots of coffee later, they were all frustrated, exhausted and no closer to having any leads on the stalker or any clue how to keep Stella LeBlanc safe. Every day that they didn't have a plan, Chance became more stressed, the furrow between his brows more pronounced.

It'd only gotten worse when another of the stalker's letters found its way into Stella's mail. Whatever the

letter contained was bad enough that Maci thought
Chance might put his fist through the wall.

She had no idea why he was taking this so personally—he hadn't seemed to do that for most of their
other cases since she'd worked here. Maybe stalking
was a sore subject for him.

And whether Chance was taking this personally or
not didn't matter. All of them needed help, so she'd
done what she could. She'd secretly ferried sustenance
of all kinds to the brothers in between her own phone
calls and office work. Nutritional snacks and meals,
since none of them were eating well.

Despite her best efforts to keep them functioning,
they all had bags under their eyes the size of Volvos,
with attitudes to match. It would have been almost
funny if she hadn't been so exhausted herself.

She'd somehow gotten some sort of stomach bug
that wouldn't quit right when the guys needed her most.
She couldn't take a sick day right now, so she hid it
as best she could. She sprayed down everything with
disinfectant and powered through.

"He could've killed her," Luke said, rubbing his eyes
as he tossed down a stack of photos from the most re-
cent stalker incident. Maci tidied them, then walked
around the table, replacing the tray of sandwiches and
bringing a fresh pot of coffee.

Chance hit play on the video images. "I don't think
that was the intent. Stella and her driver were followed
home from a local boutique she was doing a spotlight
on for her YouTube channel." He paused the video as

all the guys studied it. "See how the other car nicked the trunk? He could've done a lot more damage."

"See how the driver keeps his face averted?" Chance pointed to the image. "He knew we'd pull all photo and video footage we could get. It was a carefully constructed hit."

Chance resumed the footage, and Maci winced as the vehicle containing Stella and her driver went into a tailspin. Thankfully, the guardrail stopped it before there was any major damage.

"This is a break in the pattern," Chance said. "The first incident of actual violence."

They all watched the footage again. Then again, sandwiches and coffee ignored.

It was Weston who finally stopped it. "We need a break. Watching this on repeat isn't changing anything. Dorian has Stella on lockdown. Nothing is going to change tonight."

Luke stood up. "I concur. I'm heading home to see my wife and get some sleep. Let's meet back early and tackle this with fresh eyes."

Maci could tell Chance wanted to argue but knew they were probably right.

"I need to see my tiny terror." Brax stacked up some files in front of him. "He's running Tessa ragged."

It wasn't long before they were heading out of the conference room.

"You coming, Chance?" Weston asked.

"I'm just going to look this over one more time and then I'll leave." The brothers didn't respond to him with anything but eye rolls. If he had it his way, Chance would stay at the table until his body gave out or he found a solution. They knew better than to argue with him.

"You head out too, Maci. We'll help clean up this mess in the morning," Brax said with a mock glare and a wave.

Despite Brax's words, as soon as the door locked behind them, she started gathering up the cups from the conference room. If she cleaned it up, they'd be able to think clearer. Starting again fresh tomorrow was a good idea.

"You're exhausted. You should go home too," she said when Chance threw down the pictures Luke had been looking through.

It was the first time she caught a good glimpse of Stella LeBlanc, and she stopped in shock.

Holy hell, the woman could have been Maci's twin.

Stella had slightly longer hair in a more elaborate style, and her fashion and makeup were much more complex than what Maci wore, but they could easily have been sisters.

It was almost creepy how similar they looked.

"Yeah, I know I need to go home." Chance scrubbed a hand down his face. "But this car accident doesn't make sense. For so long, the stalker didn't change his tactics. When they stopped working, he just found new ways to get his messages to Stella. He could've gotten dangerous much sooner…so why now? What caused him to attack her like that? And in a way that's not terribly personal or inventive."

Maci forced herself to look away from the photos of

Stella. "Could the stalker have been upset about something? Maybe it was a warning."

She stacked the cups and took them to the office's small kitchen sink. She was rinsing them out, startled when she found Chance just behind her. She hadn't heard him follow her—the man could be so damned silent when he wanted to be.

But he'd followed her into the kitchen to continue talking to her. That was something.

He sat down at the small table in the middle of the room. Her entire body was aware of how close he was.

"What the stalker did doesn't feel like an emotional response. It feels like something else."

She shut off the water and dried her hands. "Like what?" She gave in to her urges and stepped closer.

As if her hand was being powered by someone else's brain, she ran her fingers through his soft hair. Chance tensed, and for a moment she thought he'd pull away. Then he relaxed into her touch, letting his head fall back to rest against her stomach. She nearly groaned, having forgotten how good it felt to touch Chance casually. The soft sigh as she scratched his scalp was enough for her to keep going.

"I don't know. If the motive was profit, the stalker would've taken her and tried for a ransom. He—and I use that pronoun because statistically that's the case, not because we know for sure—seems to want to get close to Stella, but not too close."

"Could revenge on Nicholas LeBlanc be a motive?"

"Possibly, but if so, he's moved very slowly over the

past few weeks. Maybe the stalker is just toying with her."

"That's not generally the case, right?" Maci didn't know much about stalking, but she did know that stalkers who did it just to toy with their victims were the minority.

He let out a sigh and leaned more fully against her. "Yeah. Generally, stalkers crave the emotional response the invasions of privacy forces on their victims. Someone doing it just to mess with Stella or Nicholas would be much more unpredictable."

"Maybe it's jealousy. She's successful in her own right as an influencer, so maybe someone's coming after her for that. Or they could feel slighted that she doesn't see their support for her or something. A fan who has gone a little over the edge."

Chance didn't answer, but Maci could tell he was thinking, so she didn't push. She just let him think.

"Maybe." He pulled away, then turned to look at her. "How are you doing?"

She looked down at him, brows furrowed. "Me? You're the one who hasn't slept in days."

Chance stood and cupped her cheek, running a thumb under her eye. "That may be true, but you haven't been feeling well lately either. Are you okay?"

She knew she'd pay for it later but she let herself lean into Chance's touch. Even in the middle of the week's chaos, and with things so strained between them, he'd been watching. Checking on her. "Maybe we're both working too hard."

His eyes tracked over her, cataloging everything

from her limp hair to her baggy clothes. She really hadn't been feeling great, and her look was definitely more casual than usual. She almost apologized, but he shook his head. "You should go home, Maci. Get some rest."

"I will if you will," she joked, poking him in the stomach. When he pulled her into his arms unexpectedly, she knew she should pull away, but couldn't force herself to do so. She couldn't remember the last time he'd held her, and even though her brain was screaming at her to take a step back, to walk away, she couldn't deny how well they fit together.

Of course, fitting together physically had never been their problem.

He trailed his nose across her cheek and down until it rested in the crook of her neck.

"Come home with me," he whispered. His lips were so close to her skin, but he didn't kiss her, and Maci wasn't sure if she wanted him to or not. "We can just sleep if you want, but I want you in my bed again, Maci. I never wanted you to leave."

There was no hiding the shiver that coursed through her body at his words, just like there was no hiding the gasp that came when he finally brushed his lips so softly against her skin.

Don't let your libido cloud your judgment. Think before you act, Maci Ford.

Especially since her impulsiveness was what had gotten them into their awkward situation in the first place.

But his proposal was so tempting. She wanted to

go home with Chance. She really did. She wanted to crawl into his cool sheets and fall asleep wrapped in his arms. She wanted to wake up in the morning to find him staring at her again. She wanted his hands on her after the two-month hiatus she'd forced on them.

But nothing had changed. Her mother showing up here in the parking lot a couple days ago was a reminder of that. Giving in, going home with him after so long, would make things even more muddied.

And honestly, she wasn't sure how many more times she had the strength to walk away from him. She wanted him so much.

He wanted her too. He wanted her to say yes.

She was so tempted.

But when he found out about her past—who she'd come from, the things she'd done—it would be *him* walking away.

Not just him.

Maci's breath froze in her lungs. Losing Chance would be terrible, but losing her job and the family she'd built here at San Antonio Security? That would be devastating.

She not only cared about Chance's brothers but all their significant others… Tessa, Claire, Kayleigh. Maci loved baby Walker and Sheila and Clinton Patterson too.

It was already difficult to have a working relationship when no one knew what had actually happened between her and Chance. If she wanted to keep her life and job intact, Maci had to do her best to stay away from him. Even when every part of her body was begging her to stay.

"It's better if I don't," Maci said, stepping out of his embrace even though it was agony.

He stiffened and let her go. "Okay. I'll walk you to your car."

He sounded so defeated that Maci almost took it back. She bit her tongue, holding back the words she wanted to say.

When he didn't speak either, the two silently grabbed their things, locked the door and headed into the night together. Chance stuck close as they walked across the parking lot and checked the backseat after she unlocked the doors. Once he was sure the car was safe, he opened the door for her.

"Get home safe," he said before closing her into the car. He didn't move or look away until she was pulling out of the lot. Maci slowed, watching as he climbed into his truck and drove off.

Even after she'd rejected him, he'd still made sure she was safe. He was a protector in his very DNA. A good man.

And she was definitely the wrong woman for him.

Chapter Four

Maci stepped into the office the next morning with a cup of tea wrapped firmly in her shaking hand. She'd thrown up twice before she left the house thanks to her stomach bug, but there was no way she was going to take the day off.

Not when she had a plan that could work to help with the Stella LeBlanc situation.

Chance and his brothers were already in the office, huddled around the conference room table once again. "Good morning. Is everyone feeling better?"

The guys all grunted unintelligibly and threw up random waves in her direction. To her surprise, everyone looked like they'd actually gotten some sleep—even Chance.

Someone had already started a pot of coffee in the conference room, but it was nearly empty, so she dropped her purse at her desk and started a new pot. When she looked up, she found Chance studying her.

"Our coffee not good enough for you now?"

Maci grimaced at the cup she'd set down. "Tea, actually."

Tea was nowhere near as good as coffee, but she knew there was no way her stomach could tolerate her normal brew.

Chance stood and walked over to her. "Still not feeling well?" he asked, low enough that his brothers wouldn't hear.

She shrugged. "It's a bug. It'll go away soon enough."

"If you need to take the day off—"

"I'm good," she interrupted, smiling to soften the blow. When he just stared at her, she sighed. "If I need to go home and rest, I will. I promise."

"Okay. We're meeting in ten to discuss new options on the case." Maci nodded and looked away, trying to settle the nerves in her stomach. She didn't normally offer many tactical suggestions. Between the four Patterson brothers, they pretty much had that market cornered.

She had no idea how they'd take her suggestion. But ten minutes gave her just enough time to do what she needed to build her case.

She stepped into the bathroom and pulled out her special occasion makeup. She'd watched a few online tutorials last night, one from Stella LeBlanc herself.

When she left the bathroom ten minutes later, she looked less like Maci and more like Stella.

Chance and Brax were in the same seats as yesterday, sleeves rolled up and eyes focused. Luke and Weston were poring over a tablet, pointing out things to each other. She walked to one of the conference room chairs and sat, firing up her laptop so she could take notes like she usually did. She wasn't sure when she should bring up her idea.

"Is everybody ready to officially start?" Chance asked. "We're not leaving here today until we have a plan for catching Stella's stalker. Nicholas is demanding action."

"Can't blame him for that," Weston muttered. The rest of the brothers agreed.

Brax used a remote to turn on the large-screen television near the head of the table. "Should we start by looking at the wreck again with fresh eyes?"

Once they got into that it might be difficult to drag them back out. Now was the time to tell them her plan. "Actually, before you do, I have something to run by you."

All the eyes in the room zeroed in on her.

Luke shook his head in what looked like genuine fear. "Please don't tell us you're quitting. We'll never get unburied from the paperwork."

"No, not that." Maci laughed. "I have an idea for the Stella LeBlanc case."

Luke's relief was palpable as he slumped back into his chair and heaved a breath. His aversion to paperwork was near legendary.

"What kind of idea?" Brax crossed his arms and sat back in his chair.

"Why do you look like that?" Chance asked gruffly before she could answer Brax's question. "Your makeup. It's…"

She ignored him, knowing she had to get to her point before things derailed. "I think you should employ a decoy. Someone to take Stella's place publicly to draw out the danger and eliminate it."

"You want to be the decoy," Weston guessed. Maci nodded.

A heavy silence followed, but it only lasted for three seconds before Chance exploded. "That's what the makeup is about, isn't it? Showing how much you look like Stella. There is absolutely no way we're using you."

Brax leaned forward, eyeing Maci critically. "It's not a bad plan, actually. And the makeup does make them look remarkably similar. Since Stella doesn't have a sister, that would make it even more likely to work."

"Did you hear me?" Chance glared at Brax. "I said no."

Maci took a breath to answer, but Luke shook his head across the table. She didn't argue because she could see the beginnings of a sibling "chat" brewing, and she was better off staying out of it.

"Last I looked, San Antonio Security was an equal partnership, Chance." Brax's nonchalant brush-off caused a vein in Chance's forehead to pulse. "Not a dictatorship."

Luke nodded. "We're in the business of protection. We would make sure Maci is safe. If we use her as a decoy, we'd plan it right so that no one gets hurt."

Chance scrubbed his hand down his face. "You're all out of your mind. We're not sending Maci out un-trained so we can catch a stalker."

Maci had had enough. "You aren't sending me any-where. I'm volunteering," she snapped.

Chance glared at her from his chair. "You don't know the first thing about being in the field."

"So, train her, Chance." Luke leaned forward across the table so that Chance's attention was forced onto him. "She's already more tactically aware than most civilians. She's smart and self-reliant. Give her some physical defense lessons—quick and dirty basics— and let's do this."

Chance turned to Weston, who, in normal form, hadn't yet said anything. "Will you please help me get them to see reason?"

Weston studied Maci for a long moment, then looked back at Chance. The two of them were super close. "I get why you're worried. Maci is part of the family, and we don't like the thought of any family member in potential harm's way."

Hearing Weston say she was part of the family warmed something inside Maci. Chance turned to her, and for a moment she was afraid he was going to blow the whistle on her. To explain that, since she'd snuck out of his bed in the middle of the night two months ago, maybe *family* didn't apply to her.

But if anything, Chance's gaze was more protective. More possessive. More...*everything*.

The warmth she'd felt ratcheted up to a full heat.

"It's the best plan we've come up with yet," Brax said. "Let's at least keep it on the table while we continue looking at other options."

Chance finally looked away from her and nodded. "Okay. But if we send her out, we're going to damn well make sure she's safe."

All three brothers offered their agreement.

"Stella always has some sort of bodyguards around, right?" Luke asked.

Chance let out a small sigh, as if he knew he'd already lost this battle. "Yes. She has at least three nearby at all times."

"Great," Luke said. "So, we ship the original Stella off on an international vacation, so she's out of any danger."

Weston nodded. "And also so we can control the situation more. We can send our new Stella only to events that we can have a greater measure of control over."

Brax grinned. "Plus, Maci isn't spoiled like Stella. She's an asset, not a liability. Especially will be after some defense training and running potential scenarios so she knows what to look out for."

"Fine," Chance said finally. That one word was low and gritty, like it was painful for him to speak at all. Maci's stomach swooped deliciously at the sound, and she inwardly cursed her body for responding to it. "I'll agree to this plan if you take at least three days of self-defense training with me. I'll also be with you every step of the way when you're undercover."

Maci's eyes widened. Staying in close confines with Chance day after day? That wasn't going to be easy. "I'm sure I could learn the basics from anyone. You don't have to do it all yourself."

"They've all got people waiting for them at home. You and I are the single ones of the bunch. That makes us the best people for an undercover job like this. It's me, or we scrap the plan altogether."

Chance's smile was tight. He knew she was stuck. She would always agree to anything that let the others go home to their families, but she was also desperate for a reason for her and Chance not to be alone. She had to preserve the distance between them.

She knew how easily that distance could disappear.

"What do you say, Maci?" Chance finally said. "Are you ready to work together?"

Anyone could see that he was waiting for her to say no, but she wasn't going to do it. "I'm sure it'll be a blast."

"Oh, there will be a blast somewhere," Luke muttered. Brax and Weston laughed under their breaths while Chance watched and waited. He wanted a real answer, and she could tell he wasn't going to leave without it.

Maci was simultaneously ecstatic and panicked, but she shoved it all down. Nothing else mattered but finishing the job. She had to help Stella get her life back before something—or someone—wrecked it forever.

She stared into Chance's brown eyes. "I'm in."

Maci felt like she'd just signed her soul to the devil but had no idea why.

As Maci closed up the office later that afternoon, she still couldn't believe the guys had agreed to her plan. She hadn't seen any of them for most of the day. They'd been too busy going over the plan with LeBlanc's security team, working on the details of getting Stella out of the country and narrowing down the social events where Maci would take Stella's place.

Maci was really going to do it. She was going to take an active part in capturing a stalker and making a young woman safe again. Maybe it could even count as penance for some of her own past sins.

If only that was the way it worked.

Pushing those thoughts aside, she locked the door to the office and drove to the popular Thai restaurant down the street from her place to grab the order she'd put in. A big bowl of noodle soup and too many appetizers sounded like the perfect dinner to celebrate becoming an undercover super-agent.

At least her stomach could handle it. Thankfully it had settled since this morning. Hopefully the bug was gone for good.

The last thing she needed was the flu plus three days of one-on-one with Chance. It was going to be hard enough to keep her wits about her at full strength.

Thai food would help.

She'd just put the bags on the floor of the passenger seat when her phone rang. It was Claire, Luke's fiancée.

"What's going on, woman?" Maci and Claire had become good friends when Claire had needed Luke's help a couple years ago. He and the other Patterson brothers had helped clear her name of murder.

"You have no idea how much money I would give to have seen you talk Chance Patterson into using you as bait for this stalker."

Maci winced as she put the phone on speaker so she could drive. "I'm not using myself as bait. Chance would've freaked out. I'm a decoy."

Claire chuckled. "You and Stella do look a lot alike. I still would've liked to have seen you talk him into it."

"Actually, I just suggested it and played up my makeup to look a little more similar to her. The other brothers were the ones being reasonable and listening."

"Chance is not known for his reasonableness when it comes to you."

Maci knew Claire suspected the truth. Her friend had never asked Maci outright if she and Chance had slept together, but she'd been closer than anyone else to putting the pieces together.

"Probably the most dangerous part of this entire operation will be the next few days with Chance attempting to train me. After that, a swarm of ninjas would probably be a breeze."

More laughter from Claire. "You be careful. And if it all starts to feel like too much, let someone know. Heck, you can let me know and I'll make sure Luke understands. You don't have to do anything you're uncomfortable with."

"I know. None of them would want that, even if using me is the best option. But I'm actually excited about it." She pulled up to her apartment and grabbed the bags from the passenger side.

"Good."

Maci heard some purring over the phone. "Is that my buddy Khan I hear?"

Claire's giant Maine coon acted more like a dog than a cat, and Claire loved him to pieces.

"Yeah, he's hanging here on the couch with me. I've

got awful cramps and he's my emotional support animal for the day."

"He's a good one to have. Okay, I'm home. I'll talk to you later." She disconnected the call and headed inside, hoping her own period wasn't going to make the next few days even more difficult.

She froze in the process of setting her food on the counter.

Maci couldn't remember the last time she'd had cramps.

Dread bubbled up in her stomach. Her period had been regular since she was thirteen, and for the first time ever, it was off.

"No, no, no," she whispered, swiping to her period tracking app only to groan again. She'd missed not one but *two* periods. One month she could chalk up to the stress of everything that had been going on, but two?

Two was unprecedented, and something in her gut said she was out of her depth.

Don't freak out when you aren't sure what's happening. The first step is to pee on a stick.

The next thing Maci knew, she was standing in the drugstore with no idea how she'd gotten there. She threw test after test into her basket. One test wasn't enough. It could be a false positive. That happened sometimes.

Checking out and the drive home were also blurs in her timeline. She shoved the Thai into the fridge—there was no way she was going to eat now—and dumped every test she'd bought onto the bathroom counter. She picked up a random one and opened it, shoving the rest into a very un-Maci-like pile to the side.

A quick pee and two minutes later, she was curled up with her back against the tub and the test clenched between her shaking hands.

Two lines.

"No. This cannot be happening," she told herself. "Take another one. You have to be…" Positive. The mental pun was just terrible enough to send Maci into near-crying laughter.

The next test was one of the smart tests, so when the timer went off, there were no lines, just a single word…

Pregnant.

Pregnancy had never been in her plans. She wasn't fit to be anyone's mother.

And Chance… Just the thought of him had her stomach lurching. She barely made it to her knees in time to throw up in the toilet.

He was going to think she'd trapped him. How could he not?

Now he was stuck in her life forever. After all the effort to keep him away from her, their lives were intertwined all because she was keeping this baby.

Amazing how no other option even boded consideration. Even if he didn't want anything to do with her and the baby, she still wasn't making any other choice.

You're going to be a terrible mother. You'll ruin your kid like you ruined your life.

She tried to fight back against the malicious thoughts, but she couldn't. She didn't know anything about motherhood. Her own mother used her as an ATM.

Maybe Chance might fight her for custody. Maci thought about what had happened to Brax's wife, Tessa, and how she'd briefly lost custody of her own child.

No, Chance wouldn't do what Tessa's ex had done. That had been lies and manipulation.

But maybe he would decide she wasn't worthy of his child.

There's nothing to do about it yet. Focus on the pregnancy and work—

Work. Of course, what should have been a great day had ended in such chaos. The plan for Stella's protection hinged on her and now she was pregnant. She didn't know whether to quit the plan already or...

"No. I'm doing this," she told herself, hunching over the sink to wash her face. "I'm going to decoy for Stella because she needs it, and I'm not going to worry about it. Chance will keep me safe just like he always has, and when everything's over, I'll tell him about the baby. It's going to be fine."

Maci stared at herself in the mirror and wished for the first time in ages that she had someone she could call. A real mother who could give her advice.

But she didn't have that.

She straightened, taking a deep breath. She may not have any parental figures in her life, but she didn't drink or do drugs. She was organized and clean and would do her damnedest to take care of this baby.

Feeling marginally better, she pulled out her phone and made an emergency appointment through her doctor's scheduling app for in the morning. She needed to get an official test done and check how far along she was. Then she needed to see if self-defense training was going to be a problem.

She walked into the kitchen and pulled out her food. She wasn't hungry, but not eating now wasn't an option. Then she grabbed a notebook from the junk drawer. Between bites she listed everything she needed to ask the doctor before she went to work in the morning.

She'd just follow the list, stick to her plan, and everything would be okay.

She hoped.

Chapter Five

The next morning, Chance was getting the plan ready for Maci's training when she texted about a last-minute doctor's appointment. Good. He hoped she could get some meds for that bug she had.

Or, even better, that bug would mean she couldn't take part in this plan at all.

Chance had always been logical and strategic in his thinking. That, combined with his protective instincts, had meant he'd spent a lot of time taking care of the younger kids at the group homes he'd lived in before being adopted by Sheila and Clinton.

He'd been the one to plan things out and make sure everyone had what they needed. He'd been the one able to anticipate unexpected events and pivot to plan B, C or Z.

Those logical and strategic parts of his brain knew that Maci's decoy plan was the most likely to be successful. Wasn't the fact that she and Stella looked so much alike the reason he'd been compelled to take the case in the first place? And despite the fact they fought all the time, he knew Maci was intelligent, competent and situationally aware, like his brothers had argued.

But the logical and strategic parts of his brain weren't what he wanted to listen to. He wanted Maci as far away from potential danger as possible.

And if the safest place was in his bed—*him with her*—was that really a bad thing?

But he'd agreed. He'd stand by his word and make sure she was as prepared as she could be.

Unused to the extra time, he picked up a cup of coffee for himself, adding a tea for Maci at the last minute. She could heat it up later if she wanted.

He'd rented a private room from his favorite local boxing gym. It was quiet and familiar, which was what he needed when it came to being around Maci. Being in the office with her was tough enough, but here there would be no brothers holding him back from saying things he should leave in the past.

There would be no offices to shut himself in to stop himself from demanding once again why she'd called their relationship off with no explanation.

It would just be the two of them and a few layers of cotton and Lycra separating skin from skin.

It was going to be torture.

When Maci walked through the doors, Chance could already tell she was distracted. Bloodshot eyes and bite-chapped lips were framed by messy hair, like she'd shoved her hands through it endlessly.

He caught her at the door and led her toward their training room. "How'd your appointment go? Find out anything interesting?"

Her blue eyes grew wide. "Wh-what?"

"Your doctor's appointment. Your sickness? Are you okay to move forward with this plan?"

"Oh." She forced a laugh. "I'm fine. Just a little… upset stomach. Doctor gave me a little nausea medicine, which should help."

She was lying or at least wasn't telling the full truth. He'd been studying that beautiful face and those cobalt eyes for way too long not to recognize it.

Maci was stubborn as hell and didn't like to talk about her feelings. She was blowing him off; nothing he said was going to get her to share what was really going on.

He should be used to her shutting him out by now, but he wasn't. The best he could do was ignore the burn of the slice. "Good. Then let's get you warmed up and ready to go. I got you some tea if you need it."

He led her through his favorite stretches, letting her modify them when they agitated her sensitive stomach and making a note to avoid touching that part of her body if at all possible. He wanted to train her, not make things worse.

The stretching should've helped her relax, but by the time he got her on the floor stretching her hips, she was nearly vibrating with stress.

"Maci, have you changed your mind? There's no problem if you have." There was nothing he'd like more.

"No, I haven't changed my mind." She shook her head, leaning forward to stretch her hamstrings, keeping her face averted.

He didn't like that she felt like she had to hide herself

from him. A thought struck him and he had to swallow down the lump in his throat before he could verbalize it.

Finally, he pushed the words out. "Would you like someone else to train you? If you're uncomfortable with me being here, we can swap Luke or Weston out."

It would gut him to do it, but her safety was the most important thing. If she would be more comfortable with someone else, Chance needed to step aside.

"No. It's fine. I just… I've got a lot on my mind."

"If you're sure—"

"I am. I want you to train me, Chance. I trust you." Her blue eyes pinned him.

Something eased inside him. She trusted him. She had no idea how much that meant. Hell, he'd hardly understood how much that meant until the words had come out of her mouth.

He walked her through the final stretches and warm-ups before she stood there catching her breath and waiting for instructions.

"Before we get started, let's level your expectations. I'm not going to teach you to fight."

Her face screwed up in an adorable frown. "Why not?"

"We don't have the time to get you to a comfortable proficiency with fighting. That means your goal is always going to be getting to safety. Survival is always the most important thing. Say it."

"Survival is always the most important thing."

"So, to that end, we're going to utilize your size and stature to get out of some common scenarios."

Maci stared at him with a quirked eyebrow and her

usual sassy grin. He was surprised at how much he liked seeing it. The last few days—hell, *weeks*—she always seemed to be stressed. He'd missed the sass.

"You realize I'm not exactly tall, right?"

Oh, he realized it. He gave her a grin of his own as he dragged his gaze down the length of her body, grinning wider when a hint of pink colored her cheeks.

Maci wasn't terribly short, but the fact that she fit under his chin was something he'd always enjoyed. "Exactly. Your height means that any attackers who are taller than you will have to contort their body to grab you. That gives us a small window of time to get you out and away."

She considered that and nodded. "Okay."

"We'll go through a few holds and how to break them today. Tomorrow, we'll work on escaping a few common restraints and reiterating what we learned today. The last day is basic self-defense moves that any person should know."

"It doesn't seem like a lot," she said doubtfully.

Chance agreed. "Like I said, the goal isn't for you to win a close-quarter fight. It's for you to get enough room between you and the danger to escape."

"Alright, Sensei. Teach me."

"The most important thing you have to do in any attack is keep your head. That sounds easier than it really is." And was a situation nearly impossible to replicate in training, but he wanted to mention it.

"Okay."

"You're smart and a quick thinker. Use that to your advantage."

She blushed. "Thanks."

He wasn't saying it to flatter her. "In a battle against someone stronger than you or with more fighting experience, you have to use your strengths. For you, that's going to have nothing to do with your physical muscles and everything to do with your brain."

She was listening and taking this seriously. That was good.

"Okay, let's start with a hold from behind. An attacker is likely going to wrap around you in an effort to either pick you up or hold your arms still. They won't want you to be able to fight back since this position is mostly about the element of surprise."

She nodded, taking it all in. "Okay."

He spun a finger to signal for her to turn. He then stepped behind her, forcing himself to keep focus on the task at hand and not the closeness of her body.

"If the bad guy's arms are around you, that leaves you with your legs. Go for the soft spots and try to unbalance him. Groin attacks, knee shots, anything. If you can twist your body around, you have the ability to claw at their eyes or headbutt them. Whatever you do, it's not going to look pretty, so don't worry about form. Just make sure it's effective."

He showed her the best places to kick the kneecap, and how high up on the inner thigh to aim for maximum pain if she couldn't hit the groin.

She seemed riveted as he taught her the weakest parts of the ankle and how to rotate herself so that she could slither out of his grasp. None of it was perfect, but she managed the basics well enough, and every time she succeeded, she got happier.

Making Maci Ford happy was a heady feeling. One he wished she'd let him try to do full-time.

"Alright," he finally said after they'd been at it for a couple hours. "Break free one more time and we'll move on to other things."

Chance wrapped his arms around her, hands on either bicep, but for a moment Maci didn't move and he didn't want her to. He had his arms wrapped around her for the first time in months and he was in no hurry for her to escape them again.

He tried to commit the moment to memory. The softness of her shirt sleeves under his fingers, the sound of her breathing as he kept her close to his body. He even pressed his nose to the crown of her head and took in the smell of the shampoo she loved so much. When he was sure he'd remember it for good, he squeezed her arms lightly, a reminder to focus and escape.

Maci took a deep breath and dropped her bodyweight. It was unexpected enough that he nearly released her, and she used it to her advantage. She twisted, grabbed the back of his knee and shoved her shoulder into his stomach like a football star. As soon as he was on his way down, she let go of him and scuttled to the back wall of the room.

"Perfect. That's exactly what I wanted to see. Use whatever means necessary to surprise your attacker and put yourself in a position to escape. Let's take a break for a bit then get back at it."

Chance grabbed his water bottle and did everything

in his power to focus on rehydrating rather than on Maci eating some granola bar and drinking her cooled tea on the other side of the room.

Even with dried sweat plastering her hair to her head and in shorts and a T-shirt she was damned beautiful.

How had things gone so wrong between them?

How could he make them right again?

How was he going to survive two and a half more days of being this close to her?

After the break she walked back over. She was looking a little tired, not that he could blame her. Maybe they'd take it easier this afternoon. They ran quickly through what they'd already worked on. The more it could become muscle memory for her, the better it would be.

Then it was time to move on to frontal attacks. "Alright, next up we'll go over what to do for a choke hold. In this case, you'll have eyes on your assailant and—"

He reached for her throat, but before he could connect, Maci flinched. Her whole body shifted away from him and her eyes closed. The furrow of her brow and the tight set of her mouth told him that it wasn't a voluntary response—it was some sort of unexpected reaction.

And he had no idea why she'd had it.

Instantly, he dropped his hands and stepped back. Maci had never flinched from him before. Not in the time when they'd been lovers and not when they sniped and snarled at one another.

He couldn't recall a single moment where she'd looked scared or fearful of her physical safety with him.

Seeing this flinch, even though it wasn't an extreme reaction, shattered something inside him.

"Maci? Are you okay?"

Those blue eyes popped open, and she seemed to realize what had happened. "I—I'm sorry."

"Are you scared of me?"

He hated that he had to ask, but he needed to know. "No."

"Are you sure?" Had he been misreading her all morning long, thinking she was doing okay when really she'd been hiding fear? "I don't want you trying to push through some mental block. If this training is triggering for you then—"

"It's not. I'm not scared of you."

Her voice was firm and it sent a wave of relief rushing through him, one that was almost immediately taken over by confusion. If she wasn't afraid of him, then why did she flinch? Had someone hurt her in the past?

And why the hell didn't he know the answer to that question? He barely knew anything about her past at all.

He wanted to ask. Wanted to demand to know what that flinch had been about, but knew it would lead to a fight. The real kind with them yelling at each other, not the self-defense training kind.

"I think we've done enough for today," he finally said. "Let's call it quits."

"No."

"Can you tell me what caused you to flinch like that?"

He expected her to shut him down or joke around the

question. When she remained silent, he thought maybe she wouldn't answer at all.

"My parents would sometimes get violent with each other. Both ways. I guess choking was part of it, although I didn't actively remember that until you came at me."

Chance was stunned. He'd never heard her talk about her parents. Had no idea she'd had a less than ideal home life.

He didn't talk much about his parents either. Maci had met Clinton and Sheila and knew what great people they were. But Chance had never really known his biological parents at all, so there wasn't much to say about them.

"Mace, I—"

She held out a hand to stop him. He wasn't sure what he was going to say anyway. "We're on the clock. A woman's life is at stake. I flinched but I'm fine now. Let's keep working."

"Are you sure?"

"There's a lot of things I'm not sure about, but this isn't one of them."

Chapter Six

Chance stared down at Maci in the sparring ring. Both of them were near snarling.

It was the end of the final day of training. Tomorrow she'd be heading undercover as Stella at some bigwig art gala. Whether she was ready or not.

Chance knew she was ready, or as ready as someone could get in just three days. There was so much they'd been trying to cram into the limited time. The hours of defense training may have been the most physically demanding, but all the other elements took their toll also.

Maci had spent hours studying footage of Stella's mannerisms and nonverbal communication in order to effectively impersonate her. Weston's fiancée, Kayleigh Delacruz, had come by the office to help Maci style her hair and makeup as close as possible to Stella's.

Maci, Chance and his brothers had spent an ungodly amount of time studying the people who would be at the gala, as well as friends and acquaintances of Stella's. There were a few friends—surprisingly few—who would recognize Maci wasn't Stella. Nicholas had helped make sure those friends wouldn't be in attendance—mostly by offering them a weekend trip to the French Alps.

Must be nice to have those sorts of resources.

Rich Carlisle, Stella's companion, had come in to coach Maci on how she would act with different groups of people. That entire process was distasteful. Not only was Stella basically a self-centered snob to most people, Rich was slick and handsy with Maci.

Chance had to stop himself from breaking the man's fingers every time he tucked a strand of Maci's hair behind her ear or touched her shoulder. Every time he gave her one of his charming smiles, Chance wanted to punch him in his perfect teeth.

Logically, he knew Rich was behaving the same way he did with Stella. He was trying to help the best he could. He would actually be the biggest part of selling this whole ruse—Stella rarely went anywhere without Rich.

But Chance still found his hands balling into fists way too often around the other man. Especially when Maci laughed at something charming he said.

To avoid bloodshed, his brothers had put him on layout duty—which honestly played to Chance's strengths anyway. He'd studied the layout of the gala building, determining potential places the stalker might make some sort of attempt to get near Maci. Dorian Cane had offered backup guards to place at any locations they were needed.

Chance had studied the exits and made sure Maci knew about them. And backup exits. Ignoring everyone's rolling eyes, he'd even pointed out a couple of large air shafts she could use to hide in if needed.

Long after everyone had gone home each night, he'd run possible scenarios in his head. How he would react to different threat types. How he would get Maci to safety.

Over and over. As many situations as his mind could come up with. He wanted to be as prepared as possible. It was how his mind worked. Always had been.

But now, looking down into Maci's blue eyes, he was afraid they might kill each other before the stalker had the opportunity to do any damage.

It was a stressful situation and they both were exhausted, but that wasn't really the issue here.

She was hiding something from him.

Hell, not *something*…everything. The more he thought about that flinch on the first day and what it had revealed, the more he realized how little he actually knew about this woman.

He knew they were combustible in bed. Knew that everything about her stimulated him mentally and physically.

But she had very carefully kept the details of her past from him. And the more he thought about it, the more he was convinced that it had something to do with why she'd run from his bed two months ago.

She still wanted him. And he damned well wanted her. Training so closely together over the past few days had proven that on both sides. There'd been way too many times when they'd had to take a step back from each other—both of them breathing hard and not just from exertion—to settle down.

Multiple times he'd tried to get her to talk about anything—them, her past, why she was keeping so much from him. But she'd avoided his attempts every time.

"That's it," he said, dropping his hands from her and stepping back. He'd been teaching her how to break a wrist lock, and he'd spent the entire time feeling the racing of her heartbeat under his fingers.

"What's it?" Maci asked, stepping back herself. He hated the distance. "Did I mess up?"

"No, you're doing great, but I want to talk."

Immediately, the open expression she'd been wearing morphed and he felt her shutting him out. Again.

"Let's just get this lesson done with, okay?"

"We're going to finish it, but we're going to talk too. I can protect you more effectively if you stop trying to keep silent about every personal thing about yourself."

Her shoulders tightened, creeping up toward her ears. "Chance, we've been doing so well. Just don't."

"Think about that flinch when I came at you the first time in a choke hold. It totally caught me off guard."

She shrugged. "It caught me off guard too. But we worked through it and I don't flinch anymore."

"But what if something happens while you're undercover? Something else triggers you."

"We can't possibly work through every possible scenario that might trigger me. It's impossible for anyone."

She was right. There were always internal factors at play in undercover work that could momentarily cripple even the most seasoned agent. There was no way to prepare for them all.

But this was different. His very gut told him so. "I want you to answer me one question."

Her eyes narrowed as she planted her hands on her hips. "What?"

"You're deliberately hiding something from me, aren't you. Something important."

The blood drained from her face, and he knew he'd hit his mark. Maci Ford was hiding something.

"Let's just finish the lesson, Patterson. I'm tired and tomorrow is a big day."

She was exhausted—he could see it in the bags under her eyes and the tight set of her mouth. He knew she'd been sick at least once a day despite her medication.

He should let this go, but couldn't. He had to know.

"I'll make you a deal. You break out of my hold in under two minutes and I'll leave it all alone."

"And if I don't?"

"Then you tell me why you keep saying you don't want to be with me when we both know we can hardly stay away from each other."

He saw her throat working as she gulped. "I don't think—"

Chance stepped into her space and ran a fingertip down her cheek. "I should've pushed way before now. But I didn't want you to feel like you were pressured into being with me," he whispered. "That you had to sleep with me for job security."

She blinked in shock. "I never felt that way."

"Good." They were so close, it wouldn't take much

to bend down and kiss her. He was so tempted. "I thought maybe you'd just lost interest in me, which was a blow to the ego, but acceptable. You've done a good job of hiding that you're still attracted to me, but the last couple days I could fairly taste it in the air between us. You still want me, Maci Ford."

She swallowed, drawing his eyes to her throat where he desperately wanted to press his lips, but didn't answer.

"So, if you can't break my hold in under two minutes, then you tell me why you're so damned determined to keep away from me."

"And if I don't take the bet?"

"Then I'll be knocking on your door every day until I find out the truth. Your call."

Either way he was going to get the truth.

"Fine." She took a step back, stretching her neck from side to side. "Let's do this."

Chance set a timer on his phone and gave her a three-second warning before he lunged. He kept them both on their feet, coming at her from the side to trap her arms with his own. It made it harder for her to reach him with a kick. As she struggled, Chance kept an eye on the timer.

One minute left. Maci was breathing hard and grunting with her every move. He could see the panic setting in, and he wasn't sure if it was his arms restraining her or that she knew she was going to lose. Either way, it pushed her to fight harder. Her nails dug into his stomach where they could reach and her teeth gnashed at his arms.

Good for her. It hurt, but she was using the tools they'd worked on.

Thirty seconds left. Her energy flagged, which he'd been counting on. In a real fight against someone bigger, she'd have to use bursts of speed and power.

They were down to the last twenty seconds when the gym door opened and Brax walked in with his phone in his hand.

"Hey, Maci. There's an issue at the office. We need to get you back."

They both looked over at him, and Chance's arms loosened just enough that she collapsed hard to the ground then wrenched herself away.

The alarm went off, but she'd already won.

They stared at each other for a long moment before she turned and rushed toward the locker room.

"Everything okay?" Brax asked, glancing between Chance and the door she'd disappeared behind. "You look like you need to actually spar rather than work on training basics."

There was no doubt about that. Chance's arms were nearly quivering with the need to hit something. "Let's go."

Within a few minutes they were geared up and circling each other in the sparring ring.

"What was the emergency at the office?" Chance asked, keeping a close eye on his brother. Bastard was fast.

"There wasn't one. You two were so involved in your conversation, you didn't hear me come in the first time."

Chance stopped. "How much did you hear?"

"Just the end. The bet if she couldn't break out in two minutes or less, she would tell you why she's been keeping away from you."

That wasn't as bad as it could've been, but it was bad enough. "Brax…"

"What's going on with Maci?" Brax jumped forward and threw out a cross and jab with his gloved fists.

Chance dodged the first, but took the second on his geared chin. "Nothing's going on."

Brax snorted. "Never pegged you for a liar. Are you sleeping with her?"

Chance's glove sailed toward Brax's nose, only to miss when his brother skipped out of the way. "Things between Maci and I are complicated, but no, we are not currently involved with each other."

"Currently." Brax threw another swing. "That implies that you were involved. Is that why you threw such a fit about her going undercover?"

"She doesn't know what she's doing." It wasn't a lie, but it wasn't a real answer either.

"Her risk is minimal, given the circumstances and us being glued to her every second."

"Still a risk. How would you feel if it was Tessa?"

At hearing his wife's name, Brax stopped messing around. His blows became quicker. So did Chance's. They both dodged what punches they could and took the ones they couldn't.

Eventually Chance began to withdraw. This could go on for a long time. He and Brax were too evenly matched and knew each other too well. Brax slowed down too.

"This isn't a good use of our time," Chance said. He dropped his hands. He knew his brother could get a dirty swing in if he wanted, but also knew Brax wouldn't do that.

"Agreed. We need to be firing on all cylinders tomorrow. I'm glad Maci went home. She looks like she needs some rest."

Chance just grunted as he used his teeth to loosen his sparring gloves. He was well aware at how pale and tired she'd looked.

"You going to tell me what's going on between you two?"

"There's nothing—"

"Don't lie. We've all seen the way you look at her. I just wasn't aware that it had progressed."

Chance ripped off his sparring helmet and ran a hand through his hair. "Progressed then completely stalled."

Brax shot him a boyish grin. "Maybe you should look for a girl somewhere else, man. Maci doesn't seem interested."

"I can't," he eventually answered. It was the best he could do for his brother. There were too many things unsaid for him to walk away from Maci, even if she'd already done it to him. There was too much potential between them, and Chance had never been one to squander a good thing. "I'll try not to let it mess with work though."

Brax threw him a bottle of water and they both took a sip. "I think you and Maci would be good together."

Chance sputtered his water, coughing when it went

down the wrong pipe. "But you just said to look for someone else."

"That was just a test to see if you were truly interested in her. Seems like you are."

"Are you telling me you wanted to check my intentions with her? I thought I was *your* brother."

Brax grinned. "You are, but Maci's family too, and she doesn't have anyone else to step in for her."

How the hell did Brax know more about Maci than Chance did?

Because Chance had been so caught up in the physical aspect of their relationship that he hadn't started talking to her about important stuff. He'd thought he'd have more time. That they would take it slow and get to know everything about each other.

It definitely hadn't been because he didn't want to know.

They both grabbed their gym bags and headed toward the door. Brax slapped him on the back. "I had to make sure you were ready for the long haul, because a woman like Maci Ford is a lifelong commitment."

"Don't I know it," Chance muttered. Brax laughed and changed the subject to details about tomorrow's operation. Chance barely heard him, consumed in his thoughts.

What was he going to do about Maci Ford and the secrets she clutched so tightly?

Chapter Seven

"Maci, breathe. You can do this."

She was glad for Chance's voice in her ear through the comm unit. It was the only thing keeping her even remotely grounded.

She didn't look like herself, didn't sound like herself. Didn't feel like herself.

And despite the fact that she should be focusing on this mission, her thoughts kept coming back to her pregnancy and her near-showdown with Chance yesterday.

The urge to cover her stomach made her fingers twitch, and it was all she could do to stop herself. Though she couldn't see them, all four of the Pattersons were close by. She couldn't give her secret away yet. It wasn't time.

But she knew she couldn't keep it from Chance forever. He was a pit bull when it came to solving mysteries, and she'd somehow made herself a mystery he was determined to solve.

She would tell him about the pregnancy after they caught this stalker. Right now, despite not looking or feeling like herself, she had to focus on what she was doing.

"I'm okay," she murmured into the hidden comm unit. "These are just not my normal type of people."

Chance chuckled. "I hear that."

He was in full support mode for this mission—leaving behind their personal conflicts—and she appreciated it. He'd been the one to show her how the comm unit worked and had been the voice in her ear all evening.

"Most of these people seem so fake," she murmured.

She'd known an art gallery was way out of her norm and had expected to feel out of place and generally clueless about the art. But it wasn't the art that made her uncomfortable, it was how the people were acting.

The gala was for a new contemporary artist, an in-your-face, Banksy-type multimedia creator. Maci would be the first to admit that she didn't understand any of it.

But it didn't seem to matter. The people here were less about the art and more about making sure they were seen and photographed from all different angles. Social media was the true artist here.

Rich was by Maci's side, constantly touching her—like he would Stella—but it grated on Maci's nerves. She ignored it, focusing on her smile and posing for pictures herself. They already had some pictures of the real Stella that would be superimposed over shots of the gala. Those were what would be posted online.

But right now, Maci had to be Stella enough to fool the stalker.

An hour later, despite her best attempts and Rich

all but fawning over her, Maci was convinced she was failing. Hardly anyone was talking to her.

She gripped the glass of champagne she wasn't drinking tighter. This was a mistake. She'd never considered herself a good actress even when she wasn't distracted, so why had she thought she could do this? Mingling with the elite, with their designer clothing and bejeweled shoes. Even dressed to the nines in Stella's clothes, she felt separate from everyone else. It wasn't her world and it never would be.

The urge to run, to admit her mistake and leave the room—and the case—to the professionals had her looking for the nearest exit.

"Relax, Mace," Chance told her, his voice tinny through the comm in her ear. "You look like you're going to bolt."

"I almost think it would be preferable to all of this," she mumbled into her glass.

The huff of Chance's laughter was a balm to her nerves, as was the reminder that he and the others were close by. They wouldn't let her fail, and despite the potential danger being Stella attracted, Maci couldn't help but feel safe with Chance nearby.

"Who pays this much to get in then basically ignores the art?" she murmured as Rich turned to talk to someone a few feet away.

The price tag to get in the door had been over a thousand dollars per person. San Antonio Security hadn't had to pay that, of course, but still, the thought that everyone else here had done so and then were hardly paying attention to the art…

"People who are willing to spend thousands of dollars for a single social media post," Chance answered. "Or the opportunity to network. To be seen somewhere important."

She barely refrained from rolling her eyes. The money people paid to get in here tonight could've been used for much better causes.

An arm wrapped around her waist, and lips pressed against her hair. "There you are, Stella darling."

Even knowing it was Rich and that he was supposed to do this, she had to force herself not to stiffen.

She heard Chance growl and struggled not to smile. They may have all been on the same team in trying to catch the stalker, but Chance didn't like Rich at all.

Rich was on LeBlanc's payroll even though he didn't need the money, and even Chance had admitted the man made a great secret weapon. He'd grown up in the same elite society as Stella, so it wasn't an issue for him to show up to the same events as her best friend, making him the perfect incognito bodyguard.

Or at least Maci assumed he was. She'd never actually seen him in bodyguard action, only in flirt mode. He flirted with anything that moved, including Maci. With golden hair and a tall, lean-muscled body to match, it was no surprise that his charming behavior caused people to write him off as nothing more than a playboy.

Still, Maci wished he wouldn't touch her quite so much.

Rich dipped his head, letting his breath warm Maci's hair. "You look uncomfortable. Is everything okay?"

"Fine, just needed a second. It's all an adjustment," Maci said honestly, taking a half step back to give herself some breathing room.

"You're doing great." He stopped, his arm slipping around her waist as he plastered her body to his side. "Incoming. Amy and Angelina Kendrick. Twin influencers on YouTube. They're a couple of Stella's biggest competitors. Definite frenemies."

Maci nodded, giving him a flash of Stella's signature smile, one that had taken her hours of practice in the mirror. It felt wrong on her face, but she knew she'd gotten it right when Rich winked. "You're sure they won't recognize me as not being Stella?"

"Nah. They'll want to move on quickly, get ahead of Stella in terms of photo ops and talking to important names. I can sell this."

Maci nodded.

"Ladies, so lovely to see you again," Rich said, kissing the sisters' hands and leading the conversation like he was born for it. He kept their focus on him and away from the Stella imposter at his side.

She kept her shoulders back, chin up and bored smile on her face. "Maybe you two would like to have lunch with us sometime," Angelina said. "We could talk shop."

"I'll have to check my schedule." Maci kept everything about herself loose, adopting the pretentious, distant air Stella perpetually seemed to have in public in all the footage Maci had studied.

The twins' eyes narrowed for a moment and nerves made Maci's stomach pitch and roil. Had she messed up? Said something wrong?.She wanted to look to Rich, but knew it would be a giveaway. Stella didn't look to others when making decisions, she simply made them and left everyone else to deal with the consequences.

"I'm going to get a drink. I need something much stronger than this champagne." She turned without looking at the two women and left, praying it was the right thing to do.

Rich caught up with her at the bar. "That was great! I would've sworn you were Stella if I didn't know better."

"I agree, Maci," Chance said in her ear. "You handled that like a champ."

Too bad her stomach didn't think so. It twisted and ached as Rich turned to get her a drink.

"Whoa, you okay?" He slid a drink toward her. "You really did do great. That will help sell you as Stella."

Maci couldn't pay attention to his words or the drink. All she could focus on was the nausea clawing at her insides.

Oh, no. She hadn't taken any morning sickness medicine today, since she'd felt fine this morning for the first time in a couple weeks. Evidently morning sickness wasn't limited to just the early hours of the day.

"Excuse me." She walked away from Rich, her mind whirling as she desperately tried to remember where the bathrooms were. Chance had made sure she knew where seven different exits were out of this building, but nothing about bathrooms.

Her stomach gave another lurch, and she cursed under her breath.

"Maci, you okay?" Chance asked. "Why did you leave Rich? Did he do something?"

Maci didn't want to say anything, afraid that just opening her mouth would be enough to trigger her stomach, but she knew Chance would assume the worst if she didn't. "I'm going to be sick. I need a bathroom."

She could hear Chance and his brothers talking, trying to figure out where she was going, but she didn't pay attention once she saw a sign for the bathroom. All her focus was on getting to it before she made a scene.

The relief she felt when she found the door was almost enough to send her stumbling. She shoved through, thankful there was no one else inside, although not caring if there had been, and fell to her knees inside a stall just as her dinner came up.

They really shouldn't call it morning sickness when it could happen anytime.

Maci didn't know how long she knelt there before she felt cool hands brushing her temples as they gathered up her hair, helping to soothe her overheated skin. She couldn't even be startled, could only try to remain upright as her stomach tried to empty more, even though there was nothing left.

"You're going to be okay."

Chance.

He crouched behind her, whispering soft words as his big hand rubbed soothing circles across her back.

She had no idea how she was going to explain this.

Eventually, the urge to puke disappeared and all that was left was the weariness that came from it. With one hand on the wall, Maci got to her feet, grateful when Chance's hand on her elbow stabilized her.

The first thing she did when she got out of the stall was rinse her mouth out with water and wish she had a toothbrush. Or at least some mints in her purse.

"Thanks," she muttered. She felt much better—as she always did—just weak.

"Are you alright?" Chance hadn't moved far from the stall, his arms crossed over his chest as he studied her.

She didn't have it in her to turn around and face him head-on, so she lifted her exhausted eyes to his in the mirror. "I'm fine."

"You aren't. We need to call this off."

"No."

"There will be other events, Maci."

Her eyes flashed to his in warning as she looked under the stalls. No shoes, so they were most likely alone, but still, he shouldn't be mentioning the mission.

"I locked the door behind me when I came in. We're alone."

Of course he had. The grand strategist always had a plan.

"I'm fine to keep going. It was just nerves." There was truth to that, although she knew that wasn't truly what had just happened.

She turned back to her reflection and opened her clutch, grateful for the touch-up makeup kit she'd thrown in last minute. With her makeup fixed and all signs of her bathroom interlude wiped away, she looked and felt a million times better. "How do I look?"

He took a step closer. "Are you sure you still want to do this? We can try again another night."

"I'm fine," she said. "I feel much better now."

She moved for the door, but he stepped in front of her. She could feel his gaze on her face like it was a touch, and she had to fight the urge to flinch away. Or move closer.

Those brown eyes of his were trying to dig her secrets out of their hiding spots. It was unnerving, especially when her biggest one involved him.

"The sooner we go out there, the sooner we can be done," she whispered. "The sooner Stella is safe."

He held her gaze for a moment, then another. Finally, he walked out the door, holding it open for her. "If this happens again, we're calling it."

She nodded and slipped back into the crowd.

For the rest of the night, Maci played it safe. She talked with all kinds of people, sticking close to Rich. It was Brax in her ear now rather than Chance. She thought he might be mad at her until she caught him moving around the gala with the other patrons— blending in perfectly in his black pants and shirt.

He was staying near her in case she needed him. The thought both warmed and terrified her.

By the time the gala was winding up—no sign of anything suspicious from anyone—Maci was exhausted.

"We're done for the night, Maci," Brax said through the comm. "If the stalker was going to try something he would've already done so. You and Rich head to the car, then we'll make the switch."

She was staying at Stella's penthouse apartment to further the ruse. The place was much fancier than her own, but right now that didn't matter. She just wanted a bed and to sleep for a hundred hours.

"Who has babysitting duty tonight?"

"You get me, the best Patterson brother," Brax said. "That okay?"

She forced a smile. "You know it."

Not Chance. Probably for the best. Being alone in an apartment with him would just make everything more complicated and sleep probably impossible.

But still, she couldn't stop the disappointment pooling in her gut. She liked all the Patterson brothers, but Chance was always the one she would choose to have nearby.

Even when she knew that would spell disaster.

Chapter Eight

Nothing.

Three public events over the next four nights and they were no closer to catching the stalker than they had been when Maci first went undercover. It certainly wasn't Maci's fault. She was playing the role of Stella damn near perfectly.

And Chance hated it.

He disliked seeing her face made up to look like someone else—someone not nearly as spunky and *real* as Maci. He even disliked the clothing she wore. The outfits may have been much more expensive than her normal wear, but he preferred her in her jeans and blouses over these gowns and heels.

And Rich... If Chance had to watch that man touch the small of Maci's back—the very place Chance's fingers itched to be—much longer, he wasn't sure he could be responsible for his actions.

"Any sign?" Chance asked his brothers.

"None." Brax's frustrated voice matched his own. "Is this guy playing with us?"

"I don't know." Chance rubbed the back of his neck.

Tonight he was in the control room and Brax was out on the floor as immediate backup for Maci should she need it. He and his brothers had taken turns, so no one would remember seeing them at other events.

The pattern had been the same. They showed up, Maci played her role remarkably well, and they studied everyone around her. Anybody who talked to Maci got checked. Hell, anybody who'd looked in her general direction got checked.

Dorian Cane and his team had provided assistance—checking identities and running unknown people through facial recognition software. Dorian himself had sat in the control room with Weston yesterday in case he might recognize anything they were missing. As an experienced security professional who kept his ego out of the situation, his presence had been appreciated by all of the Pattersons.

But still nothing.

"I think maybe the stalker is on to us and knows Maci isn't really Stella. To continue to parade her around isn't going to change anything," Chance said.

They'd already had this talk with Dorian. He had upped the security on Stella in Europe, although there hadn't been any suspicious events there either.

"I agree," Weston said into the comm unit. He was positioned at the staff entrance near the back of the building. "There's something we're missing. Guy is ahead of us."

There'd been nothing at each event, nothing as they followed Rich each night as he drove Maci back to Stella's apartment, and nothing as she stayed there for a couple hours before sneaking out a private basement entrance to go home.

Even worse than the nothing was the strain the situation was putting on Maci. Each time, as the hours wound down, she was slower to move, her smile a little less bright. By the end, she was exhausted and nearly weaving on her feet despite being completely sober.

Chance had had enough. "Maci's done," he said into the private channel only his brothers could hear. "Let's call it."

"Roger that," Weston responded. "I'll go make sure the apartment is clear."

Chance could hear the exhaustion plain in his brother's voice too, so he made a decision for them all.

"No, you all head home and get some rest once we get Maci to the car. I'm going to let her go home rather than go to Stella's apartment. Luring him out isn't working, so tomorrow we need to figure out a new plan."

None of his brothers argued. They all knew this wasn't working the way they'd hoped.

"Call if you need anything," Luke said. "We won't be far."

Chance switched over to the channel Maci could hear. "Maci, we're calling it quits for tonight."

On the screen, he watched her turn discreetly so she could talk to him without anyone noticing. "We're heading back to the apartment?"

"No. For whatever reason, this method isn't working. I'm going to take you home. Everyone needs a good night's sleep."

He watched her rub her eyes. "I feel like I let you down."

"No, don't say that. You've been a stellar Stella."

He watched the corners of her mouth turn up at his horrible joke. "I wish it would've worked."

"Don't worry. We're going to get him. You and Rich start to move toward the car."

Brax agreed to stay and watch until the end of the event and oversee packing up all equipment. Chance met Rich and Maci in the parking garage. Maci was already inside the car.

"Giving up?" Rich asked.

Chance narrowed his eyes. "Maybe for tonight. No use beating a dead horse."

Rich's smile was full of charm. "I try not to get beat ever. Let me know what the next step in the plan is."

Chance watched Rich saunter away before getting in the driver's seat of the car. He looked over to ask Maci how she was doing.

She was fast asleep, cheek leaning heavily against the door. He stared at her for a long moment. They'd definitely made the right choice by ending early tonight. Enough was enough.

Chance didn't drive fast. Maci needed the sleep and at least here he got to be close to her. She was still keeping secrets he wanted to get to the root of. Maybe if she wasn't actively part of the investigation he could focus on that—something he'd been thinking about since that last day of training.

But maybe instead of trying to crash through her walls, he needed to try to *gentle* his way through them.

Not his strong suit, but he would try. She was worth trying that for.

They were only a few minutes from the party when Chance noticed a car that seemed to be following them. Not wanting to wake Maci without reason, he took a roundabout way that led them back toward Stella's apartment. If someone was following them, that's where they'd expect the car to be going.

At a red light, Chance made a last-minute turn, hoping the car would simply drive on.

It followed.

Nerves prickling at the back of his neck, he continued to drive around in a circle. Each turn he made, the car did too.

Definitely following.

"Maci. Maci, wake up."

"Are we there yet?" her sweet, sleepy voice asked.

As much as he hated to do it, she needed the truth. "We're being followed."

Her head jerked up. "What do we do?"

He dialed Weston on the car's speakerphone. "We're okay. Just stay low."

"What's wrong?" Weston answered his phone with the question.

Chance rattled off their location. "Black sedan is following us. As soon as I spotted them I headed toward Stella's place to keep them on us."

"On our way." Chance could hear the squeal of tires as Weston spun his car around. "Luke is with me."

"I need to get Maci into the apartment. I want to take this on the offensive."

Maybe it could all end tonight. There was nothing Chance wanted more.

"I'll just stay in the car with you," she said. "You don't have to drop me off."

"No." There was absolutely no damned way. If this turned into something ugly, he didn't want her anywhere around it.

He slowed down just slightly to buy them more time. A few lights later he turned again and the car followed.

"We're blocks behind you," Weston said. "Luke sees the sedan. They're definitely following you. We'll block them while you drop her off."

A few moments later, Weston smoothly cut around and in front of the sedan, blocking its view just as Stella's building came up on the right.

He looked over at Maci as he stopped the car. "Run inside. Don't stop for anyone. Get into the apartment and lock the door. We'll be back as soon as we can."

Thankfully, she didn't argue. "Be careful."

Chance watched until the doorman let her in the building, then pulled away fast. He got a glimpse of the black sedan as it sped past his brothers' car, and watched them lurch after it.

"I think they're on to us. They're speeding up." Weston told him. "We're heading south on Market."

"Stay with them. I'll be caught up to you in less than a minute."

"Damn it," Luke said. "They just turned south on Fourth, heading toward the interstate. They're trying to lose us."

Chance was less than three blocks away. He jerked

the wheel in a sharp right into an alley, hoping it would allow him to gain speed and cut off the sedan. "I'm coming in hot from the east in a parallel alley."

"What's your plan?" Weston asked.

"Get in front of them and make them stop."

"That's a terrible plan," Luke and Weston said at the same time.

It was the only one he had.

He gunned the engine and pulled out of the alley. He'd done it—the sedan was speeding toward him.

"We see you!" Luke yelled.

They were now in the more industrial section of town, which worked to Chance's advantage—there was little other traffic at this time of night. He positioned his car in the middle of the street so there was no way to go around it, then got out.

He spared a moment to wonder if they'd try to ram his car, but the car slammed to a halt instead. Chance's brief flare of relief died when not one but two doors opened, the people inside the car bailing and running in opposite directions.

Luke and Weston squealed up behind them.

"I'll get the driver," Chance shouted, taking off in a sprint. "You get the other one."

The driver ran back through the alley Chance had just driven through, trying to get back to the main street. Chance had to stop him before he did that. He forced speed from his legs, gaining on the smaller man. Finally he leaped, hitting the man in a flying tackle, taking them both down.

They both hit the ground hard, but for the first time

since he noticed the sedan, Chance felt like he could breathe.

Finally.

He dragged the man back through the dark alley to the cars, glad when he didn't put up much of a fight. Luke and Weston had gotten their perp too. From the light of the streetlamp Chance finally got a look at the pair.

Holy hell. They were *teenagers*.

He looked over at Weston and Luke and realized they were thinking the same thing.

It had been damned *teenagers* stalking Stella Le-Blanc?

"How old are you?" Chance demanded.

"Seventeen." The driver tipped his chin up defiantly, and Chance could see the rosy edges of his eyes.

"What's your name?"

The kid rolled his eyes. "I'm Bert." He hooked his thumb toward his friend. "This is Ernie."

Chance's jaw tightened, but he let it go. They would get IDs later. He looked closer at the boys' red-rimmed eyes.

"Are you high?"

That didn't make sense. How had a stoned kid managed to slip past so many layers of security over the past few weeks?

"Who wants to know?" Ernie asked with a smirk.

Chance crouched down beside them, ignoring the question. "Why were you following us?"

Bert scoffed. "We're not telling you anything."

"Fine." Luke took a step closer. "We'll call some

friends of ours with the San Antonio PD and get you transferred to lockup. Harassment, speeding, DWI. You broke enough laws that they could take your license permanently. And seventeen is old enough to go to real jail for a couple of nights. Maybe you can make a few friends. I hear they like fresh meat."

Both boys paled. "Look, we didn't want to hurt anyone."

"So why were you following Stella LeBlanc?" Weston asked.

"Who?" Bert asked. "We don't know who we were following."

Ernie shook his head, looking like he was about to pee his pants. "Yeah, someone paid us to follow your car and make sure you knew we were doing it. We didn't think you'd get all psycho!"

Chance met eyes with Weston. This didn't make sense. "Start over. What exactly did they pay you for?"

"Just to follow the car. They said you'd probably find us, so we should keep the chase going as long as we could."

"Who?" Luke took a step forward, scaring the kids even more.

"I don't know!" they both shouted.

Chance grabbed Bert by the collar. "Who hired you? A man? Woman? What did they look like?"

Bert started shaking. "A man. We were hanging out outside the convenience store, and he offered us five hundred dollars to mess with you guys when your car pulled out of the garage. He stayed in the dark. I didn't see him."

"Why would someone do that?" Weston asked. "He didn't pay you to hurt or chase a woman who would be in the car?"

The boys shook their heads. "No, not hurt anyone. Just follow and be sneaky."

Chance looked over at Weston, his stomach sinking. "They were a distraction. I sent Maci inside alone."

Alone in an apartment that the stalker had already proven he could get into.

Chance was moving before he'd even finished his sentence, sprinting to his car. He could hear his brothers talking to each other about who would stay with the kids, but didn't care.

He drove as fast as he could back toward Stella's apartment building, dialing Maci's number as he went.

No answer.

Not the first time he called. Not the second. Not the third.

A couple of miles had never seemed longer as he drove at reckless speeds. Finally, he pulled up to the building and left the car illegally parked at the front.

The doorman stared at him as he sprinted to the elevator and pressed the button for the penthouse. Anxious energy prickled across his body, his fingers twitching as the floors passed in no time.

Maci was okay. She had to be okay. She'd been so tired. She'd probably fallen back to sleep.

Why didn't he believe that?

The second the elevator doors opened, he knew he was too late. The door to Stella's apartment was cracked open. Lock the door, he'd said. He didn't know if Maci had even had a chance to try.

Please let her be alive. He pulled his gun from under his jacket and pushed through the door.

Please let her be alive.

The stillness of the apartment made the hair on Chance's neck stand up. He wanted to call out for Maci, but he didn't want to risk alerting anyone that he'd arrived before he was in place to take them out. He quickly and silently glanced around the living room, then headed down the hallway toward the bedrooms.

He heard a slight noise behind him and spun back with his weapon raised. He lowered it when he saw it was Weston.

Weston gave him a brief nod, his own gun in hand. Without a word they both moved silently down the hall. Chance cleared the guest bedroom; Weston cleared the office.

Where was Maci?

She wasn't in the master bedroom or any of the bathrooms. Had she been taken?

They made their way back out to the living area. When he caught sight of her foot lying limply on the floor of the kitchen in the doorway, he dropped all pretense of silence and ran to her.

If it wasn't for the cut on her forehead, he could've believed she was just sleeping right there in front of the dishwasher. Ignoring the blood, since head wounds always bled a lot, Chance dropped to his knees beside her. His fingers shook as he searched for a pulse.

Please. Please. Please.

"Is she—" Weston didn't finish.

A pulse. Thank God. "She's alive."

Chance pulled out his phone, and his voice cracked when the operator asked about his emergency. "We need an ambulance."

Chapter Nine

Maci woke slowly to the sound of steady beeping and the realization that she wasn't where she was supposed to be. Before she could figure out why, the incessant tone stole her attention again.

Had she left on an alarm?

"Make it stop," she croaked. Her mouth was dry and her voice sounded weird. She heard rustling nearby and forced her eyelids open, wincing at the bright light. Lights too bright for her apartment or Stella's. "Where am I?"

"You're in the hospital." Chance. Just the sound of his voice was enough to help calm her.

At least until she looked at him. Stubble lined his cheeks, and his eyes were bright red with exhaustion. His dark hair stood up on end as if he had been running his fingers through it for hours.

Then his words hit her. *Hospital*. Instinct had her hands flying to her stomach to protect the baby. Was something wrong? Had she lost it?

Did he know?

"Are you going to be sick?" He stepped closer, then paused at her side.

"No. How long have I been here? Am… I okay?"

"Two hours. You've been in and out the whole time." Nervous energy crackled around him, and Maci wasn't surprised when he started to pace. "You got hit on the head in Stella's apartment. Do you remember that?"

The apartment. Getting inside and deciding to make some tea.

The man.

"There was a man inside Stella's apartment," she whispered. "I didn't see him."

Her breath hitched. All that self-defense stuff she'd done with Chance and she'd never even had an opportunity to use it.

Chance reached for her hand, squeezing it. "It's okay. You're safe now."

A nurse walked in. "Awake for good this time, it looks like. How are you feeling?" She shined a small light in Maci's eyes and had Maci follow her fingers with her eyes.

"My head hurts, but otherwise I think I'm okay. Is everything okay?"

Maci had no idea how to ask about the baby with Chance in the room. She looked nervously over at him.

The nurse caught her look. "Do you want to be alone? We let Mr. Patterson in because he was listed as your emergency contact, but some people feel like they recover better on their own."

Maci shook her head, then stopped at the ache. "No, it's okay. I'd like Chance to stay." She didn't want to be alone right now.

The nurse smiled. "Your pupils are responding well

and you're quite coherent—both good signs. Dr. Ashburn will be in soon and will probably want a CT scan to see if we're dealing with a concussion."

"Have I had any bleeding or anything, um, not on my head?" Maci wasn't sure how to ask about her pregnancy outside of stating it outright. "Any other problems anywhere else in my body?"

The nurse smiled. "Everything else looks fine. You're young and healthy."

That didn't answer the question exactly but reassured her a little.

The nurse left and Chance sat down next to her.

"I'm so glad to see you fully awake and talking. When Weston and I found you in that kitchen…" He scrubbed his hand down his face.

"The guy was already there when I came in. He had to have been waiting for me."

"Are you okay to talk about it or do you want to just rest?"

She let out a sigh. "I'm okay to talk. I know that will help with the case."

His eyes met hers. "The case isn't as important as you and how you're feeling."

She couldn't look away from him if she tried. "I'm okay to talk about it. I promise."

"The guys are out in the waiting room. Do you mind if I bring them in or is that too much?"

"It's okay."

He stepped out and a few moments later came back with Brax, Weston and Luke. All four brothers looked pretty haggard.

"There she is." Brax rushed over and kissed her on the cheek. "Thank goodness. Luke was out sobbing over having to file paperwork himself."

Luke grunted with a smile. "That's not completely untrue. We're glad you're okay, Maci."

Weston, solemn as always, nodded. "You gave us quite a scare."

"She's feeling up to talking about what she remembers, before the doctor comes back in," Chance said.

He sat back down next to her and grabbed her hand. It gave her the strength she needed to tell what had happened.

"You dropped me off and I rushed upstairs. I was so nervous the whole way up, but I knew once I saw the door, I was okay. I got inside Stella's apartment and locked it, but he must've already been inside."

Chance squeezed her hand and she concentrated on that.

"I went into the kitchen to grab some tea and he came up behind me. Pushed me against the wall and told me he knew I wasn't Stella."

"Did he say anything else to you?" Chance asked.

"Yeah. But his voice was weird. A low whisper." She grit her teeth. She was never going to forget how his voice sounded, how terrified she was, the words he said. She dropped her voice in an imitation of his. "How stupid do you think I am? I know you aren't her. A pale imitation of the real thing. Then again, there's strength in you. You stayed to battle while she ran. There's honor in that."

She looked at each of the Pattersons. "Those maybe weren't the exact words, but it's pretty close."

"How did you get hurt?" Weston asked quietly.

"He shoved me into the cabinet and I hit the knob." Maci remembered the pain of hitting the sharp metal, the warmth of blood dripping down her face. The man had scoffed at it, and when she lost her balance, he let her fall. "When he saw me bleeding, he let me go. I don't even remember seeing him leave. I passed out. I don't know if he meant to take me or not."

"He might have but then once you were hurt it changed his plans. Harder to hide in plain sight with a bleeding woman." Brax's frown said he didn't like the idea.

"Maybe worried about a blood trail leading us to him?" Luke guessed.

"He may have gotten word from the driver that we'd caught up to them." Weston and Chance looked at each other, but neither looked convinced. "We'll take a look at surveillance around the apartment and see what we can find."

A knock interrupted and an older woman in a white coat stepped in. "Hello, Maci. I'm Dr. Ashburn. It's good to see you awake and alert."

She did the same routine as the nurse, shining a small light in Maci's eyes and having her follow the finger.

"We did an initial CT scan when you first came in and that showed very minor swelling—good news. Your tox screen and blood work came back normal."

"CT scan?" Maci could feel herself tensing. "Could that be…bad for me?"

The doctor seemed to understand what Maci was truly asking about and shook her head kindly. "CT scans pose very minimal risks."

"I had CT scans all the time when I played sports in high school." Brax knocked on his head. "I wasn't great about avoiding concussions, but a CT scan was never any issue."

"Everything about you is just as healthy as it was yesterday," Dr. Ashburn said. "Except for the bump on your head."

"Is there anything we need to look out for?" Chance's fingers tightened on Maci's briefly, but he kept his focus on the doctor.

"Other than signs of a worsening concussion, no. The cut is superficial. It won't even need stitches. The butterfly bandage will keep it closed so it heals on its own."

"Should we watch her overnight or something?"

As much as she liked how protective he was, Maci didn't need Chance focused on her. It would be so much harder to hide the baby. "Chance, I'm fine."

"But what happens if—"

"Chance." He looked at her, and Maci saw the fear that drove him to nearly smother her. She'd been hurt on his watch and he was suffering for it. She squeezed his hand softly. "I'm fine. Tell him, Doc."

"We'll send you home with instructions for the next few days, but all in all, Ms. Ford is fine. She's in great health." She turned to Maci. "You don't need to be concerned about anything but your head. Okay? Everything else is fine."

But Chance wasn't letting it go. "What about the fact that she's been throwing up multiple times over the past few weeks? She's exhausted all the time and is crazy sensitive to certain smells. Even the flu shouldn't last this long. Plus, sometimes she seems fine and then it just comes on her without warning."

She squeezed his hand. She'd had no idea he'd been paying such close attention. "Chance, it's okay. I'm okay. Let's just worry about the concussion and getting this case solved."

He brushed a strand of hair back from her forehead. "You're here at the hospital. You might as well let them run some tests or whatever. If something is wrong with you, let's find out now. Find out early. Whatever it is, I'm here."

"Dr. Ashburn said my bloodwork came back normal. I'm okay."

He leaned closer, his brown eyes pleading. "Mace, you and I both know something is wrong. Let them check you over while you're here. What if it's cancer or something like that?"

"I don't have cancer."

"How do you know?" he whispered. "I've been watching you suffer and I can't stand it anymore."

She had to tell him. It wasn't ever going to get easier. "I'm not sick, Chance. I'm pregnant. About ten weeks along."

Chance's eyes got big, but thankfully he didn't let go of her hand.

"And I can attest that the fetus is fine, even despite the bump to the head," Dr. Ashburn said. "Maci, let me know if you have further questions. We'll do one more CT scan, then release you if everything looks good."

The doctor said goodbye to everyone and headed out the door, but Maci couldn't focus on that. All she could focus on was the raw shock on Chance and his brothers' faces.

Her secret was out.

PREGNANT.

The word kicked around in Chance's brain. *Maci is pregnant.*

Had she known when she made the suggestion that she go undercover?

Was it his?

That question stuck around the longest. Was the baby she carried one they'd made together? They'd used protection, but it wasn't always perfect. Birth control failed and condoms broke. The how wasn't the issue, the *who* was.

Who was the baby's father and what would Chance do if it wasn't him? He and Maci had no commitments to each other—although that hadn't been by his choice.

"Give us the room, guys."

His brothers knew him well enough not to argue in any way.

"You owe me ten dollars," Luke muttered to Brax as they left. "I told you there was no way there wasn't something between them."

Weston was the last one out, laying a grounding

hand on Chance's shoulder. "Be gentle, brother. She's been through a lot tonight."

He didn't say anything as Weston left and shut the door behind him. If there was any word that didn't fit the way Chance currently felt, it was *gentle*.

Off balance, amazed, fearful, angry… But not gentle.

Although he would find it. He knew right now that was what Maci needed, so he would find it.

Maci adjusted herself in the hospital bed, and it brought Chance's focus back.

"Is it mine?" For some reason, he couldn't look her in the face when he asked, so he stared at his lap instead. "You and I never had any commitments, so I don't want to assume…"

"Yes, it's yours. I haven't been sleeping around with a bunch of people."

Now his eyes flew to hers. "I didn't mean it that way at all. Truly. I didn't think you were involved with anyone else, but I thought it would be more rude just to assume the baby was mine."

She nodded, but he felt like an ass when a tear leaked out of her eye and she wiped it away quickly.

"I'm sorry," he whispered.

"It's okay."

Holy hell. Maci Ford was pregnant with his baby.

"Are you keeping it?" He tried to keep this as neutral as possible too. He refused to influence her decision, but he was flooded with relief when she nodded.

He was going to be a dad.

For minutes, neither of them said anything, Chance

just trying to take it all in. Then his brain restarted and suddenly he had dozens of questions.

"How long have you known?"

Maci looked away, and his blunt fingernails dug into his palm. He wasn't going to like this answer. "A few days."

"A few?"

She turned back to him then, the fire that was normally so bright in her eyes nothing but embers. She looked tired, and Chance had the urge to wrap her in his arms while she slept, but he had to get some info first.

"I found out for sure the day before we started training."

The last-minute doctor's appointment. Fear and anger tightened Chance's throat, and he had to take a deep breath just to curb them. His voice was rougher than gravel when he spoke. "You did all that training and went undercover knowing you were pregnant."

He thought back to the moves he'd taught her. None of them should've affected her belly area at all, but he hadn't been taking extra care like he would've if he'd known.

And then the attack tonight…

There was guilt all over her expression and in the way her shoulders slumped. "The doctor said it was fine. I specifically asked about the self-defense training, and he said at this stage I was fine as long as I wasn't taking direct hits to the stomach. He said even then my body would work to protect the baby even at risk to myself."

That barely made him feel better. "You went under-cover on a case where your doppelgänger was getting stalked by a newly-violent offender while you were pregnant with my child. Tell me you understand why I'm having an issue with this, Mace."

"I promise you, I was being careful. You guys were there to—"

"You were attacked!" The need to move pushed Chance out of his chair. "You're sitting in a hospital bed, hurt."

"That isn't fair. We both know this isn't my fault." Chance's heart dropped to his stomach. She was right. It wasn't her fault, it was *his*. He'd left her to go up-stairs alone, certain he was needed somewhere else.

He'd left her defenseless.

His whole life had been spent taking care of others, and then one mistake had nearly cost him Maci and their child. What would've happened if he hadn't got-ten back in time, or if the stalker had decided to take Maci with him?

What if he'd decided to kill her right there in that kitchen when he found out she wasn't Stella?

For a moment there wasn't enough oxygen in the world.

"Chance, stop it," she snapped. She snatched his wrist, yanking him back into his chair. "This is not your fault. You didn't know that the stalker was wait-ing for me, and who knows if you being there would have actually helped. He might have killed you."

"You can't know that." He sat back, a bone-deep

exhaustion pulling at him. So much more than from just a sleepless night.

"I'm okay. The baby is okay. That's all that matters."

That was true, but he still couldn't shake the terror wrapped around him. "No more undercover. You're done."

Maci's eyes widened at his tone, only to narrow into slits. "You don't get to command me, Chance Patterson. I'm not yours to control."

"Like hell am I allowing the mother of my child to work in a situation that's already proven to be out of control. It's not happening." Maci opened her mouth to respond, but he continued. "Besides, your cover is blown. You said it yourself…the guy knew you weren't Stella."

"Then you ask me. You don't demand."

Chance's jaw was tight. He drew on every bit of love and respect he'd ever seen between his mom and dad. Clinton and Sheila had some fights, but in the end, their respect and admiration for each other won out over any arguments.

He grabbed Maci's hand gently, grateful when she didn't snatch it away. "Maci, your cover is blown. If it was any of my brothers I would say the same thing. We need to regroup and come at this a different way. Please help us do that."

"What about Stella?"

"She's still out of the country. Between us and her other security team, we'll keep an eye on the situation and find the stalker before she comes back in the country. She's safe, we've got time, but you going undercover is no longer viable. Agreed?"

Maci sighed. "Agreed."

That took one problem off Chance's list. Now only a thousand more to go.

Chapter Ten

After another round of vital checks and a clear CT, Dr. Ashburn agreed to release Maci. While the rest of his family went home to grab some sleep, Chance stayed so he could take her home. The shock of learning about the baby hadn't worn off, but his trepidation had.

His brothers would spend the bulk of tomorrow following up on what happened tonight—finding out what they could about Bert and Ernie and checking all the footage from the apartment building. He trusted them to handle it thoroughly, because he wouldn't be there.

Maci was pregnant with his baby, and he was going to be there for them both. Whatever it took. He'd already sent Weston by to get a bag of his clothes and necessities, because he wasn't going to leave Maci alone. Not today. Not tomorrow. If he had his way, not *ever*.

The sun was starting to come up as they got her discharged and wheeled out to the car.

"What's with the bag?" She nodded to the duffel in the back seat.

"Clothes for me. I'm taking you home and I'm going to stay with you for a few days."

She let out a small sigh. "Chance, this isn't necessary. The stalker isn't after me, he's after Stella. I can take care of myself."

"That's all true, but I want to be there anyway." He sighed, running a hand over his face. "It's been a rough twenty-four hours, and I'd just feel better if I was close to you. You and the baby. Is that okay?"

She looked like she was going to fight him until she caught sight of his face. Something in his expression convinced her otherwise. "Okay."

"I thought you were going to fight more on this," he admitted with a laugh.

"I know Dr. Ashburn wants to make sure I'm monitored for a while. And you're right. We've all been through a lot the last few days."

It wasn't until Chance put the car in Drive that he realized he didn't know where she lived. They'd spent nights at his house and days together in the office, but he'd never gone to her place.

Not that he hadn't wanted to. It was just how things had always ended up. Was that part of the reason she hadn't wanted to immediately tell him she was pregnant? Part of the reason she stopped wanting to see him a couple months ago? She thought he wasn't interested in her life?

"Uh, I don't know where you live."

She nodded then gave him directions as he drove. The farther they went, the more Chance's frown grew. It wasn't the worst area of town, but it wasn't anywhere he wanted Maci and their child to be. When she directed him to pull into an older apartment's parking lot, he tried to refrain from making any comments. The window frames drooped with water damage, and the squat buildings themselves had definitely seen better days.

Maybe he could convince her to move in with him before the baby came. It would be a tough sell, but he would try. Even as uncertain as everything was, he wanted the three of them to be a family.

In the meantime, he'd stay with her wherever she was.

He found a spot close to the doors and helped her out of the car—despite her grumblings that she wasn't an invalid—giving her space once she was steady on her feet.

They made their way to her apartment silently, with Chance taking everything in and Maci watching him. She seemed to shrink the closer they got, like she was embarrassed.

"It's not pretty, but it's home."

He shrugged. "I've lived in worse places."

Hell, he'd spent most of his childhood in worse places.

"Yeah?" She glanced at him as they rounded the final bend in the stairs. Chance tried not to read into her expression too much.

"Yeah. I didn't always live with Clinton and Sheila. Some of my group homes left a lot to be desired. So yeah, I've lived in worse places than this."

"Me too," she said quietly, stepping into the hallway and leaving him to trail after her. For a moment, he couldn't.

Had Maci Ford grown up like he and his brothers had? Had she been forced to grow up too soon, to take care of herself when no one else would? Had her home situation been something no child should have to go through?

And why hadn't he ever asked?

She'd had him listed as her emergency contact, for God's sake. Didn't that state a lot about her relationship with her family?

He was so lost in his own thoughts he didn't realize Maci had stopped in the hallway not far from her door.

"What's wrong?" Out of instinct he wrapped an arm around her waist and pulled her behind him. But other than a middle-aged woman standing in front of one of the doors, he didn't see anything amiss.

"Going to introduce me to your friend, May May?" the woman asked, her eyes traveling over Chance's body. While he didn't like her ogling him, he could definitely see a resemblance between her and Maci.

"Mom." Maci stepped around and in front of Chance and moved to the door. Her knuckles were white as she gripped her keys. She definitely wasn't excited to see the woman standing at the door. "What are you doing here?"

"Can't a mama come to visit her only child every once in a while?" She looked at Chance again. "Aren't you going to introduce me to your friend?"

"No."

That was it. Just no. Maci's mom looked irritated but not surprised. It was easy to see in the way Maci kept her eyes angled toward her mother that she didn't trust the woman. Chance stepped closer to her on instinct.

Maci unlocked the door and shoved it open. She moved to step inside, but he grabbed her arm.

"Can I clear the apartment first?"

Maci nodded. Without another word, he stepped inside.

The one-bedroom apartment was just as small as he expected, but neatly furnished. Everything looked well used, but it was tidy and clean. Pops of vibrant colors bled through the white-on-white color scheme, reminding Chance of Weston's gardens. It was beautiful and homey, just like Maci.

He took his time clearing each room, even going so far as to check the window locks. There were a few things he'd do to up the security of the place if he couldn't convince Maci to move in with him.

Once he was satisfied that the apartment was clear, he went back out to Maci and her mother. The two were talking to each other in low, tense voices. They stopped when he approached.

"We're clear."

"I need to talk to my mom for a minute alone."

He had to fight the urge to push himself into their conversation. Maci looked tense and almost scared. This definitely wasn't a good relationship.

But pushing now wouldn't do him any favors. They had to learn to trust each other, and there was no better first step than giving her the space she needed. "Okay. Are you hungry?"

He almost slipped and mentioned the baby. That

would've been a huge error, given the nonverbal interaction between the two women.

"I could eat. Grab whatever you want to eat or drink too," Maci said, nodding toward the kitchen with her chin as she gripped her mother's arm. Maci practically dragged the woman into the bedroom without a single glance back.

Chance tried to think of logical reasons that Maci would be so detached from her mother, but nothing good came to mind. The desperate need to do a background check on Maci's mom pressed against him until his skin felt tight, but he wouldn't. Not without Maci's permission first.

If she wanted him to know about her past, she would tell him.

Though it was a solid reason, it still chafed—especially knowing the woman was his child's biological grandmother. The reminder that they'd eventually have to tell his own mother filtered through his brain, and he actually smiled. Sheila Patterson loved children, and she had been not so subtly hounding his brothers for more of them since Brax's son, Walker, entered the picture.

She was going to lose it when she found out Maci was pregnant. The two of them had met quite a few times since Maci started working for San Antonio Security.

Finally, the ladies came back. Maci looked even more tense, but her mother was smiling.

"See you soon, May May!"

Maci didn't respond and she definitely wasn't smiling. The second the door closed on her mother, Maci collapsed onto the threadbare couch in the living room. As suddenly as she dropped, she was on her feet pacing again.

He cleared his throat, gathering her attention. He pushed the sandwich he'd made toward her over the counter, but she shook her head, obviously too wound up to eat.

He wanted to push. This was part of the secrets she was keeping and he wanted to know. But when he looked at her, Chance could see the exhaustion setting in. It had already been a traumatic night, and the strained relationship Maci had with her mother was taking a further toll.

He pushed the sandwich toward her again. "I'm not going to pry, but I'm sorry having your mother here made things more stressful."

Maci rubbed at her eyes. "Mom has a gift of making everything more stressful."

"Does she show up a lot?"

"More than I'd like."

That didn't tell him much, but it gave him an idea. "Would you like to come home with me instead of us staying here? It'll be a lot calmer there, plus no unexpected visitors."

He held his breath, fully expecting her to say no. And if she did, he'd honor it. But at least at his house he felt like he could better protect her.

Even from foes he didn't even know she had.

"Yes, please."

No arguments. No complaints. Nothing. Chance

couldn't help the grin that spread over his face, one that got bigger when she let him hold her hand. "Let's pack a bag and take you home then."

Chapter Eleven

Maci woke up the next morning in Chance's guest room feeling much better. Her head still hurt, but not as bad as it had. Plus, she didn't have to worry about going undercover as Stella anymore.

Most importantly, she didn't have to pretend like she wasn't pregnant. It was okay if she got sick, okay if she needed to sit down, okay to be completely overwhelmed. She didn't have to hide it.

Chance had taken the news much better than she'd thought he would. She definitely hadn't expected him to want to stay with her. If she could've thought of a reason to tell him why she shouldn't go back to her apartment, she would've done it.

She wasn't embarrassed by it, per se. But compared to his place, hers was pretty run-down. Everything was clean, but secondhand. The place fairly screamed that Maci was barely on her feet financially.

And then Evelyn being there… Maci rubbed her eyes. It could've gone much worse than it had. Once she'd gotten her mom back to the bedroom, she'd offered her all the cash she had on hand to leave.

Long-term, it wasn't the best way to deal with Evelyn. But Maci hadn't been thinking long-term. She'd just wanted Evelyn out before she revealed all Maci's sordid secrets—or the few she was sober enough to remember.

At least Evelyn wouldn't be showing up here. That was the most immediate reason why Maci had agreed to stay at Chance's house when he offered.

She'd slept most of the day, so there hadn't been much chance for them to talk. She knew he must have questions. She was less sure whether she had answers for any of them.

When they ate dinner across from each other, it was mostly silent. Chance's life had changed practically overnight, and she wanted to give him time to digest everything. He deserved a second to breathe. Truthfully, she wanted the time too.

She wouldn't avoid the big conversations forever. She just needed a second to get her bearings.

When Chance sat down on the same couch she'd curled up on after dinner, Maci knew her time was up.

"We should talk—" he started, only to be interrupted by a knock on the door. Frowning, he turned to her. "Were you expecting anyone?"

"Nope." Especially not here.

She stayed where she was as Chance headed toward the door, grabbing his weapon from the gun safe as he did. She heard him let out a sigh.

"Open the door, Chance! We want to see your baby mama." Claire's voice was muffled through the front door, but Maci could still hear her friend's cheerful pep.

"Incoming," Chance muttered, then opened the door.

It wasn't just Claire, Luke's wife. It was also Brax's wife, Tessa, and Weston's fiancée, Kayleigh.

"We wanted to come over and see how Maci was doing," Kayleigh said. "You know, have some girl time."

"Right." Chance met eyes with Maci from behind the women, eyebrow raised. He was making sure she was okay with company. She knew without a doubt that if she said she wasn't ready, he'd kick the girls out, even if it meant taking flak from his brothers for it.

His protectiveness did something to Maci. She'd never had someone care about her like that. She gave him a nod, letting him know it was okay. She knew her friends had questions, and she owed them a face-to-face talk.

He followed the women as they gathered around Maci. "Can I get you all something to drink?"

Maci hid her smile behind the blanket. Despite not having them their whole lives, Sheila Patterson had raised her boys right. The impeccable, gentlemanly manners proved it.

"No, no. We're fine." Tessa pointed at Maci. "We just want to talk to this one."

He nodded. "I'll go back to the other room and call the office. I'll get an update on what's been happening."

Maci knew he'd already done that today, but appreciated him giving them time alone. "Thank you."

As the others got comfortable, Chance disappeared into the kitchen again. When he came back, he dropped a sleeve of crackers, some ginger ale and a trashcan in arm's reach of Maci. When she arched an eyebrow, he grimaced. "In case you start feeling sick. Need anything else?"

Well, swoon.

Aware of everyone watching them, Maci shook her head and thanked him. Chance looked her over again and leaned down to press a kiss to her forehead. "Yell if these three get out of hand."

As soon as the home office door shut behind him, all three friends started talking at the same time.

Claire let out a sigh. "I hope Luke acts like that when I eventually get pregnant."

"That was the most romantic thing I've ever seen." Kayleigh fanned herself.

Tessa crossed her arms over her chest. "So, you and Chance? You're a sneaky one, I'll give you that."

Claire nodded. "We all knew you two needed to get together, but we had no idea you already *had.*"

Maci let out a sigh. "We were casually seeing each other a while ago."

It wasn't quite the truth, but it wasn't a lie either. They had been casual, but their time had mostly been spent wrapped up in one another.

"And you aren't anymore?" Kayleigh asked.

"I broke it off." Even that made her cringe. She hadn't broken it off, she'd ghosted him as much as she could with them working together. Suddenly, the half-truth didn't feel right in her mouth. "It was just sex."

"Not anymore," Claire quipped, grunting when Tessa nudged her in the shin. "So, why'd you break up?"

"I'm not the type of person someone like Chance should settle down with."

Kayleigh frowned. "Why not?"

Maci's past rushed through her mind, fragments of moments she barely remembered. Ratty mattresses and worn-down people. Broken bottles and dark, desolate places. Bad decisions that haunted her. Most days she used them as fuel to make a better life for herself, but sometimes they served as reminders of how far she could fall.

But her friends didn't know about her past either. "Let's just say that my history doesn't make me a good candidate for someone like Chance for a serious and long-term relationship."

"Who cares about your history?" Tessa frowned. "We've all got a past. All that matters is right now. You're a good person, Maci Ford. You're hardworking and kind and loyal to a fault. Anyone would be lucky to have you, especially Chance."

She knew Tessa was just being a good friend, but every part of Maci disagreed. Chance needed someone better at his side. Someone stronger and with far less baggage. Maci could fill an entire closet with hers.

"Did Chance demand long-term and serious?" Claire asked.

"No, but…" Maci couldn't finish. She'd cut Chance out of her personal life before he could even get close to that point.

"No, but you were afraid he'd go there," Kayleigh guessed.

Maci nodded. She'd intentionally tried not to dream of a future with him, but every time they gave in to their off-the-charts chemistry it became harder. She knew if he'd started talking about commitments, she'd never have the strength to deny them both.

Claire shook her head. "So, it's not that you're not with him because you don't have feelings for him. And I already know he has feelings for you."

Maci definitely had feelings for Chance Patterson. "It's complicated, you guys."

"It always is." All three women said it at the same time, then laughed.

"Can't be any more complicated than Brax and I," Tessa said. "He thought I was Walker's nanny, not his mother."

Claire shrugged. "Luke wasn't sure if I was a murderer at first."

Kayleigh grinned. "I thought Weston was the groundskeeper, not my bodyguard."

Maci couldn't help but smile herself. "I guess it is always complicated."

"So, what are you going to do?" Tessa asked.

"About what?"

Claire squeezed her hand. "About the baby, about Chance, about everything. You have the opportunity to point things in the direction you want them to go."

"Chance and I are going to be coparents and maybe friends. That's it." Even if she was the one who had to draw the line between them. Chance was always protecting her, and this was her chance to protect him for once.

"Uh-huh," Tessa said. "Do you still want to be with him?"

Yes. It wasn't even a question. Maci wanted everything with him, she just wasn't sure that she could have it. So, once again, she took the coward's way out. "I don't know."

Kayleigh called her on it, eyebrow raised. "Yes, you do. You just don't want to admit it."

"I already said—"

"We know." Kayleigh rolled her eyes. "You're not a good fit. You'll drag him down. Blah, blah, blah. Have you ever asked Chance what he wants?"

Tessa moved to sit on the coffee table directly in front of Maci, grabbing her hands tightly. "Instead of trying to protect him, why don't you let him make his own choices? It's what you would want if the roles were reversed."

She winced. "But he doesn't know—"

"Then tell him." Kayleigh squished onto the table with Tessa, setting a hand on Maci's knee.

Claire slipped an arm through Maci's and suddenly they were all connected. "Chance is a big boy who knows how to weigh risk and rewards. He's capable of choosing whether he stays or goes and in what capacity he wants to be in your life, but it's unfair of you to take that choice from him."

"I'm scared. I don't want to hurt him."

"You already have," Claire said softly, grimacing when Maci flinched. "I don't say it to make you feel bad, but you have to know. Pushing him away when anyone can see that he wants to be closer is hurting him. Especially when he has no idea what he's done wrong."

"He hasn't done anything wrong."

"So, tell him that. Talk to him. It's okay to be scared, but you two are going to have to find a way to coexist for the rest of your lives. Wouldn't it be better to do it with a clean slate?"

Maci didn't even have to think about it. The girls were right. Chance deserved to make his own decisions, but how could she tell him everything he needed to know? How could she give him the reason he needed to walk away from her?

And how would she survive once he did?

"You don't have to do it right now, but just think about it. Okay?" Tessa pulled Maci off the couch and into a hug. "We're here for you."

"Anytime, anywhere," Claire added, snuggling into Maci's back.

"Whatever you need." Kayleigh slid an arm around her waist.

Wrapped in her friends' arms, she heaved a deep breath for the first time since she found out she was pregnant. Tessa, Claire and Kayleigh—because of their connection to the Patterson brothers—had become pillars of her life and the best friends she'd ever had.

They were just pulling away when Chance came out of his office. "I can come back if you need more time."

"Actually, we're heading out." Tessa pulled Maci back into a hug, whispering, "Let him make his own choices."

After the others said goodbye too, she ushered them out the door.

Chance closed the door behind them, but didn't move. He stood by the entryway and stared at Maci.

Something in the way he watched her made Maci feel almost vulnerable, and she wrapped an arm around herself as if the added barrier would help.

"What are you doing?" she finally asked.

"Looking at you."

Uncomfortable under his gaze, she fell back to her default snark. "Obviously. Why are you doing it?"

"Because you're beautiful."

Maci opened her mouth, but nothing came out. What was she supposed to say to that? The air thickened around them as the silence grew, and suddenly it was too much.

"I'm sorry," she blurted.

Chance's brows lowered, shadowing his eyes. "For what?"

"I should have told you about the baby. I should have told you—" She cut herself off. It wasn't the time to invite her demons into the conversation. Not yet. They'd have to talk about them eventually, but that was a problem for future Maci.

"Why didn't you tell me?" His tone held no malice.

She walked back into the living room and plopped back onto the couch and looked down at her lap, twisting her fingers over and over. Finally, she decided that if they were going to have a chance at coparenting—*or more*—she had to be honest with him. They'd never be able to be anything if she kept hiding the truth. Baby steps.

"I was scared."

"Oh, honey." Just like that, he was kneeling at her

feet, big hands cradling her face. "What were you scared of?"

Nothing. Everything.

She wanted to tell him, but she knew she couldn't. He didn't need to see how big of a mess she was. Eventually it would be clear, but for now, she wanted him to never stop looking at her the way he did. Like he cherished her. Like he understood her. Like he wanted to know every thought she ever had.

As if he could read her mind, he leaned in so close that their breath mingled. "You don't have to tell me right now. There's no rush." He pressed a soft kiss to her lips, the barely-there touch making them tingle. "Keep your secrets for now, Maci Ford. I'm not going anywhere."

Maci's chest ached at the tenderness in his voice and the way he held her. As she reached for him, pulling his face to hers, she knew that she was already gone. There was no avoiding the path back to each other that faith had put them on.

She wasn't optimistic enough to believe they'd have forever, but for now, she'd enjoy having Chance at her side again.

They kissed slowly, eventually moving to Chance's room where they relearned each other's bodies. Every kiss, every touch, stoked the need that months of distance had created. Maci's skin burned, aching for more with every sweep of his hands, and when they came together again, the look on Chance's face was like nothing else.

His eyes spoke his truth in waves of reverence and

awe. The way he touched her, the way they moved together, felt a little like worship.

When they were spent, Chance curled his body around hers with his hand resting protectively on her stomach, his lips pressed softly to the nape of her neck. The steady counts of his breathing lulled her to sleep, and though she told herself not to fall for the dream, for the first time since she'd run from him, Maci felt at peace again.

Chapter Twelve

For the first time since he and his brothers had opened San Antonio Security nearly five years ago, Chance didn't really want to be here in the office.

He'd left Maci curled up in bed and hadn't wanted to leave this morning. She hadn't wanted to let him go either, but he was pretty sure it was more because she wanted to get back to work than because she would miss him.

Promising to bring home dinner from her favorite Italian restaurant if she took the day off to rest had finally worked. She'd agreed, though she'd glared when he suggested spending the day in bed napping.

He chuckled. Maci wasn't someone who enjoyed a lot of idle time. The food bribe had worked today, but he had no doubt it wouldn't work for long. Especially since she felt guilty that he was going out of his way to get it.

He didn't mind. He liked taking care of her. *Wanted* to take care of her. Wanted to make up for lost time when he hadn't taken care of her.

Chance had spent the morning holed up in his office,

mostly because he needed to catch up on the intel his brothers had been gathering while he'd been gone. He read about Bert and Ernie—real names Daniel Neweth and Miles Dary—although official questioning of them hadn't led to much more info than what they'd said the first night. Someone had paid them; they didn't know who nor had they seen a face.

Dead end.

He also spent time writing up the report for Maci's attack and the car chase. He forced himself to tamp down the terror that still wanted to overwhelm him just at the thought of finding her lying so still on the floor. And that was before he'd known she was pregnant. He got the report done and sent it out.

But the real reason he was hiding in his office was because he knew his brothers were waiting to pounce. They wanted the details about Maci and the baby.

He couldn't avoid *the talk* forever, but he could avoid it for now. They were scheduled to meet Nicholas Le-Blanc today for an update.

By the time Chance came out of his office, it was past lunch and time to leave for the meeting.

"He lives!" Luke joked, but slid him a travel mug of coffee and a deli sandwich. "Thought we were going to have to smoke you out to get you in the car."

"Just trying to get caught up on everything. Especially paperwork."

Luke's pronounced shudder at the word made Chance laugh into his cup. Coffee in hand, the pair found their way to the SUV out front where Brax and Weston were already sitting.

"So, Maci…" Brax said as he drove. "She feeling better?"

Chance hoped this wasn't the start of the inquisition. "No residual issues from the attack. She's feeling tired and sick, but said it's just normal pregnancy stuff."

He took a sip of his coffee and made a note on his phone to pick up a pregnancy book or two. "I promised to grab food on the way home if she'd just stay home and rest."

Home. He'd let himself drift off to the idea of walking through his door after a long day and finding her in his house more than once. It was almost too much for Chance, especially when he'd woken up that morning with her hair on his pillow and the utter certainty that she belonged there. With him and their baby. Always.

"Good. Let's get this meeting over with quickly," Weston said. "The sooner we finish this, the sooner you can get home. No one wants to make a pregnant woman wait."

His brothers let it go with that—no further questions. Chance shouldn't have been surprised. They wouldn't push if he wasn't ready to talk. Especially when they needed to be focused on the case at hand.

They parked at VanPoint Tower and headed up to Nicholas LeBlanc's office, finding him with both Dorian Cane and Rich Carlisle.

Chance tried to hide his distaste for Rich as best as he could, but all he could see was the other man's hands on his Maci. It left a sour taste in his mouth.

LeBlanc shook everyone's hands, despite the obvious tension surrounding him. "Dorian let me know about your teammate's injury. The woman who was impersonating Stella. Will she be alright?"

"She's recovering, but we won't be using that style mission anymore." There was no way in hell Chance was allowing that. "Her cover was blown anyway, so it's a moot point."

"That's a shame." Rich's charming smirk covered his face, as always. "I enjoyed spending time with her. She's feisty."

Chance's hands clenched into fists at his side. It was only Weston's hand squeezing his shoulder that helped him remain focused rather than leap across the room and knock the smirk off Rich's face.

Dorian stepped forward. "Did the teenagers who were paid to get you to chase them provide any usable intel?"

The idea that teenagers had been paid to send grown men on a car chase throughout the city didn't sit well with any of them. What if they'd crashed? What if they'd hurt someone?

"Nothing." Luke shook his head. "No phone number or contact information for the person who paid them. They never saw his face."

"We have contacts with the San Antonio PD so we called it in with them," Weston continued. "Kids were brought to the station, but they ultimately were only held for driving under the influence."

While his brothers talked, Chance kept his eye on Rich. Chance's dislike was definitely personal, but it was also more than that. Something about the man was beeping all over Chance's threat radar.

Rich's background check had come back clear when they'd run it, but something still felt off.

"How much did the guy pay them?" Dorian asked.

Weston shrugged. "Enough to get high a few times. That's all they cared about."

"So, you have an injured employee, we have two teenagers who are useless for providing info, and we are still no closer to finding Stella's stalker," Nicholas said.

Chance grit his teeth. The other man was correct in his summary of the situation. "Yes. Using a decoy isn't going to work anymore. Before knocking Maci unconscious, he told her he knew she wasn't Stella. We don't know when or how he figured it out."

"We know he knew where all the security cameras were in your daughter's apartment," Brax said. "He took out the one in the elevator completely and was able to avoid the hall and lobby cameras."

"Even the ones we set up in secret?" Dorian asked.

Chance nodded. "Guy kept his head tucked down and face averted for everything. Avoided the cameras but didn't seem to know where they were specifically beyond the elevator. Doorman didn't see anyone, so he came in through the service door."

Dorian looked as frustrated as all of them felt. It was like the stalker was always one step ahead of them.

And even worse, he was starting to escalate. No more letters and two violent instances in a row. When stalkers changed their MOs so abruptly, it could spell disaster for the object of their obsession.

"Stella isn't happy about keeping out of the lime-light this long," LeBlanc said.

Brax quickly shook his head. "Coming back now could be the worst thing she could do. The stalker obviously doesn't know where she really is because there's been no attempts on her in Europe."

The rest of them, including Dorian, were quick to agree.

"Mr. LeBlanc, we're still committed to solving this case," Chance said. "Doubly so, now that the stalker hurt one of our own."

LeBlanc rubbed the back of his neck. "What's the next step then?"

"We'd like to look through the footage for the last few months of events to see if there are any guests or patterns that we can discern. We'll need a full accounting of Stella's schedule to match up the times she got the stalker's letters we've already got at the office."

"Full staff list too," Weston said.

Rich shifted slightly in his seat. He looked uncomfortable. Was he nervous? Bored? Hungover from going out last night? All were possibilities.

"We've got all the security footage already. I'll get that for you," Dorian said. "I'll make sure to include who was guarding Stella and her apartment as well."

Chance nodded, glad the other man wasn't offended by them wanting to double-check his work. "If we continue to work together, we'll catch this guy. Everybody makes a mistake at some point. We'll figure out a way to hurry that along."

Not long after, with the meeting over and a plan in place, the Patterson brothers headed home. No one spoke until they were pulling away from the building.

"Rich didn't like that we're investigating the past," Weston said.

Chance tapped his fingers on the seat next to him. "No, he didn't. He especially didn't like that we're going to have full access to the staff list."

"Could he be the perp?" Luke asked.

Chance shrugged. "It wouldn't make much sense. He's had unfettered access to Stella for years. Why start being a pseudo stalker at this point?"

His brothers all murmured their agreement.

"Who wants to bet money we're going to find him doing something shady on the footage?" Luke asked.

No one was dumb enough to take that bet.

"For now, let's just focus on the plan," Chance said. "We look through the footage and dig through employees and people closest to Stella. We look again at the people who message her or follow her obsessively on social media. I think whoever it is has to be someone close."

"Why do you say that?" Weston asked.

"They know too much to just be watching. This feels like intimate knowledge."

"They could have a mole in the staff," Luke suggested, writing the idea down on his phone's notepad for later.

They all let out a groan.

"Don't say that," Brax muttered. "That'll make our lives indefinitely harder."

Chance scrubbed a hand down his face. "We have to consider the possibility."

A mole would have enough knowledge to evade

them for a long time, and all he wanted to do was clear this case up and concentrate on Maci. He didn't have time for chaotic stalkers when he had a baby on the way.

They made it back to the office and everyone started to pack up for the day. Funny how Chance wasn't even tempted to try to talk his brothers into staying late and working.

Having someone at home waiting made all the difference.

"I'll see you guys tomorrow."

Brax stopped him with a hand at his chest, pushing him back toward the office kitchen. "We've cut you some slack with the questions of what exactly is going on between you and our beloved office manager."

Luke smiled. "But there's no way in hell we're leaving here without a toast to our new niece or nephew."

Weston wagged his dark eyebrows. "And to you becoming a father, ready or not."

Luke pulled out a bottle of whiskey—the expensive one they used very rarely. "This is usually for celebrating big wins. I think Chance becoming a daddy is the biggest win of all."

With a grin at Chance, he poured them each a drink, and all four of them lifted the glasses in a toast.

"Chance," Brax started, "fatherhood is the wildest ride with the most amazing reward." He was the only one of them able to speak of fatherhood with intimate knowledge. "I know you're going to ace it."

Weston clapped him on the back. "You've been fathering everyone around you since we all became Pattersons. Probably did it before that too. That's how we know you're going to be so good at it. You've got a lifetime of practice."

Luke held his glass up and they all joined. "Congratulations on becoming a dad and making us all uncles again. To fatherhood!"

"To fatherhood!" They clinked their glasses and sipped.

Once again it hit him. *He was going to be a dad.* Maci was having his baby.

"So, Maci, huh?" Luke waggled his eyebrows, making Chance laugh.

"Yeah. It was…unexpected."

That really made his brothers laugh.

"Only to you," Brax said, shaking his head. "It was plain as day to anyone else with working eyeballs, despite the hostility you both threw. Tessa and I had a bet on when you'd get together."

Though he was curious, Chance decided he didn't need to know who won in the end.

Brax nodded. "You and Maci aren't a surprise. It was inevitable."

"Maybe," Chance conceded.

"So, are you two together now?" Luke asked. "Should we add another place for family dinner this week?"

"We'll see about dinner. Depends on how she's feeling." He finished the last of his whiskey. "And no, to us being together. At least, I don't think so."

Luke's eyes sharpened on Chance's face. "You can still be part of the child's life without being romantically involved with Maci. Do you want to be together?"

"I do." The answer was immediate. Chance knew

months ago he wanted her as more than whatever they were. She'd just run before he could admit it. "Maci is... Well, you know her. She's great. She's funny and smart as a whip. I love how she keeps me—keeps all of us—on our toes. I like how easy it is to rile her up and that she can throw back whatever I dish up. We just fit."

"Have you told her that?" Weston asked.

He let out a sigh. "No. She's skittish. It feels like she's two seconds away from bolting at any given moment." Like she'd done the first time.

"I'm no expert on relationships or women, but why don't you start by telling her that? Maybe it'll help, let her put down some roots. It's hard to be real with someone when they aren't sure where you stand."

Chance knew Luke was right, he just didn't know how to tell her.

There was something fragile about Maci, despite her prickly exterior. She could argue and fight with him all day, but something still made him want to protect her even from herself.

"You're probably right," Chance admitted. "But for now, I've got dinner to pick up."

He headed out of the office, already looking forward to getting home to his girl, whether she knew she was his or not.

Chapter Thirteen

Maci lasted three days cooped up in Chance's house.

And while she loved the closeness the two of them had shared, she was ready to get back to work.

"Be reasonable," Chance said, snatching the sweater out of her hand and throwing it back onto the bed. "You just got out of the hospital."

She picked up another sweater and pulled it on, only to realize it was Chance's. She debated taking it off, but it was too comfortable. Dressed, she faced him again. "Three days ago. I'm fine, Chance. I'm not an invalid."

"You need more rest. So does the baby." He crossed his arms over his way-too-sexy chest.

But if he thought bringing up the baby—or crossing his arms over his chest like some supermodel—would help his case, he was wrong.

"The baby needs a mother who isn't bored out of her skull, especially since I'm not planning on being homebound for the entirety of my pregnancy. Besides, I have things to do at the office."

"One more day. Relax here for just one more day."

Maci had done nothing but relax for days. She was

done. She looked him over with narrowed eyes. His casual work clothes weren't the suits he wore when bodyguarding, so she knew he was likely doing desk work. "Are you doing anything dangerous in the field today?"

He frowned. "No."

"You guys scoping out another hostage situation?"

"No." His jaw clenched and she smiled. He already knew he was on the losing side of this argument.

"So, why can't I go into the office?"

Petulant silence. It was almost enough to make Maci laugh.

"That's what I thought. I heard you talking to your brothers about going over the party footage today. That's desk work. I can help with that."

"Maci…"

"I'm not made to sit around and eat bonbons. I need something to occupy my time or I'm going to go nuts and start redecorating this house to look like a ninety-year-old cat lady threw up everywhere. I'm talking doilies and lace on every possible surface. Pink walls. The works."

He stared at her and Maci could tell he wanted to argue, so she went for broke.

"Please, Chance. I don't want to fight. I just need to get out of the house. Plus, I was there at those parties. My insight might be useful."

He sighed, running a hand through his hair. "Fine, but only for a few hours, and if I see even a single wince, you're leaving and you'll stay home tomorrow."

Maci didn't bother to hide her giddy smile. She hopped across the room and popped a kiss to his cheek. "Deal!"

STEPPING INTO THE office after so long away was like coming home for Maci. She'd missed the soft gray walls and warm wood. Even the sticky note reminders everywhere put her at ease.

Seeing the mess the brothers had left in the kitchen was far less enjoyable.

"Did we get rid of the dishwasher while I was gone?" She raised an eyebrow at Luke, who was in the process of leaving his dirty cup in the almost-full sink. He froze, eyes wide when he saw her hovering in the doorway.

"I forgot?"

"I'll just bet you did," Maci grumbled. Luke wisely loaded the dishwasher before turning back to her.

"Didn't know you were coming in today, Maci."

"That's because she should still be home resting," Chance said from directly behind her. He'd barely given her an inch to breathe since they walked in the door.

Maci waved his words away. "Ignore him. He's annoyed because he lost the argument."

"I didn't lose the argument. I chose to stop fighting because you asked me to."

That took the wind out of her sails. He was trying. Chance was overprotective of everyone on his best of days. Her pregnancy certainly hadn't quelled that behavior in any way.

He didn't like her being here, but he was *trying*.

She made herself some tea and found her way to her desk. It wasn't until she pulled out her chair to sit that he spoke again. "What are you doing?"

"I have hundreds of emails and dozens of invoices to

get through. Thought I would get started doing the job you guys pay me for." Maci turned on her laptop and waited for it to boot up.

When she glanced up, Chance was back to scowling. It wasn't fair that he was so handsome when he brooded. "We're all working in the conference room."

"It's easier for me to work out here."

"I want you in there."

She wasn't about to delude herself that it was because he wanted to be near her. Nurse Chance just wanted to micromanage her choices.

"I've only got a few hours in the office, at your request, so I'll work here where I can actually get things done."

She moved to log in and Chance pulled her chair back, spinning it so she faced him. "It's not a request, Maci. You wanted to come back to work and I'm respecting that—"

"I hardly consider badgering me at every opportunity respecting anything."

"—but I'm going to keep an eye on you while you're here. I know you won't tell me if you're hurting, so consider me your shadow until it's time to go."

Now it was Maci's turn to glare. "You going to follow me to the bathroom too?"

"If I have to." He didn't look a bit like he was bluffing.

Maci debated arguing more. That's what they did, argue. Chance didn't have any right to tell her what to do with her time or her body, she knew that. But she could see the furrow in his brow and the tenseness in his shoulders.

He was *worried* about her.

The attack had scared him, and now that he knew about their baby, he was doubly afraid. What was the harm in letting him coddle her a bit longer? Especially since she had every intention of moving back into her own place soon.

"Fine. I'll stay in eyesight, but so help me, if you really follow me into the bathroom, I'll be using those defense moves you taught me to take *you* down."

He kissed the top of her head, then moved her things into the conference room, greeting the others. She pretended not to notice as he brought in extra water and snacks for the table as well, knowing they were actually for her.

And definitely didn't let her heart get all gooey at it.

While the brothers talked about the case, Maci put in her headphones, falling into her spreadsheets and files with easy bliss. She'd missed her desk job. Missed answering emails and doing paperwork. It suited her much more than her single attempt at undercover work did, that was for sure.

She dug through the backlogged emails, sending invoices to clients and vendors, and getting caught up on everything the guys had let slide the last few days. By the time the scent of takeout filled her nose, she was feeling pretty tired and hungry, but the sense of accomplishment she'd been missing filled her with joy.

Chance rapped his knuckles softly on the table at her side. She pulled out her headphones, and he nodded to the white foam boxes everywhere. "Time to eat. You've been in the zone for hours."

"Perfect timing. I'm almost done." With a few more keystrokes, she finished her last email and sent it off. Shutting her laptop, she moved everything to the side and grabbed the container Chance set in front of her. Chow mein with extra sauce and egg rolls. Perfect.

"This is so good." Chance smiled at her as he and the others pulled their usual orders out of the bag. It didn't escape Maci's notice that he'd gotten her food out first.

The guys were mostly quiet as they ate. "Anything with Stella's case?" she asked.

Chance stabbed a piece of meat with his fork. "We've been going through party footage from the last two months trying to find any repeats or patterns that we didn't notice before."

Luke ate a big bite of ramen. "So far, we've got nothing. No leads, no patterns, no suspicious faces. And the boys we chased were a dead end—they didn't know anything. Nothing on Stella's apartment security feed either."

She pushed her food away from her, not feeling as hungry. "I guess I was pretty useless too."

Chance pushed the food back toward her. "No. You survived and are healthy and whole. That is definitely not useless."

"Would you mind if we ask you a few questions about the voice you heard?" Weston asked.

Chance turned and glared at him. Obviously, Chance had told them not to ask her about it.

Enough was enough. "Yes, please do. I want to help if I can."

"You don't have to," Chance muttered.

She rolled her eyes. "What harm exactly do you think is going to come to me by trying to remember how the stalker sounded?"

"I don't want it to upset you."

She folder her arms over her chest. "You know what upsets me? Possibly being able to help stop a stalker but someone deciding for me that it's too much, rather than allowing me to make my own decisions."

There were snickers around the table but she kept her eyes on Chance.

He gave in with ill grace. "Fine."

Now she turned to Weston. "What do you want to know?"

"Did you recognize the voice at all? Or maybe there was some sort of accent or noticeable trait?"

"It was a weird, spooky whisper. Like he was trying to be menacing." As if him breaking into the apartment hadn't been menacing enough.

"Do you think it could've been anyone you talked to at one of the events?" Brax asked.

She shook her head. "Not that comes to mind."

"What about Rich?" Chance asked.

"Rich?" Maci turned to Chance. "Do you think it was him?"

"We aren't sure. We're trying to eliminate all possibilities."

Maci thought back to the attack, to the voice echoing in her ears. "I don't think so. Rich's voice is warm all the time. The man who spoke was cold. Empty."

Lifeless. The man who grabbed her had sounded lifeless.

"But then again, it was a sick whisper," she continued. "I've only ever heard Rich's regular voice. But still, I don't think it was him."

The brothers glanced at each other. Chance frowned again. "Alright, so not Rich. Could you pick the voice out if you heard it again?"

"Yes." Maci knew that for certain. "It's not something I'll ever forget."

"I know you didn't get a look at his face, but what about smells or strange sounds?" Brax asked. "Anything you can remember will be helpful."

She tried to think back, but other than the voice, everything else was a blur. "I'm sorry."

"Would you mind if we try something, since he was behind you?" Weston asked.

"Sure."

"Stand up for a second." Weston offered her his hand to help get her to her feet. "Okay, so think of the voice, when the guy was behind you."

She nodded.

Weston looked over at Chance. "You go stand behind her."

Even knowing it was Chance, that she was completely safe, she was already tensing.

"Where did you hear the voice when he was behind you?" Chance asked. "Think about it. Was it high above your head, like where I am now? Or maybe a little lower."

She closed her eyes and forced herself to really think about it. "Lower. Closer to my ear."

She opened her eyes, not wanting to relive that any longer.

"So could be someone around five foot ten," Weston said. "Someone as tall as Chance would've been higher."

That made sense.

"But the guy also could've been leaning in toward her," Brax pointed out.

Maci sat back down in her chair but didn't reach for her food. She'd definitely lost her appetite.

"I'm sorry I'm not more help."

"It's fine. You're doing your best." Chance rubbed his thumb across her knuckles. "Why don't you help us look through some footage for a bit? Your half day is almost up anyway."

He was giving her an out and she was beyond grateful for it. "I'm going to come back tomorrow. Do you even know how many emails came in while I was gone?"

"We're supposed to check emails?" Luke joked, wincing.

They got out the footage and she pulled the screen closer. Maybe she'd be more useful this way. But as minute after minute scrolled by, she didn't hear or see anything that reminded her of the man in the apartment.

It was mind-numbing to sit there and watch it all. She had no idea how the guys did it.

She was only an hour or two in before her back was a tangle of knots and everything hurt. She leaned back in her chair and grimaced at the sharp ache in her muscles. Of course, her nursemaid saw and immediately swooped in.

"Alright, you're done," Chance said, ushering her out of the building and into his SUV, barely giving her time to grab her things and say goodbye.

She didn't even argue. She was exhausted.

And even worse, she hadn't been useful at all.

Chapter Fourteen

Chance arrived at the San Antonio Security office the next morning, coffee in hand, glad he'd been able to talk Maci into sleeping late and working a half day in the afternoon. She could talk tough all she wanted about how she wasn't an invalid. But the truth was her body had been through a trauma with the attack and was already exhausted from the pregnancy.

His phone pinged with a reminder as he stepped inside the building and he smiled. Maci had an ultrasound the next day and he was going.

The thought that they'd be able to actually see their baby—at least the heartbeat—had Chance shaking his head.

He was going to be a dad.

"You are a godsend." Brax snatched a cup of coffee from Chance's tray, gulping half the drink down in one go. "Walker is in the middle of sleep regressions. I was up most of the night."

Brax's two-year-old son was technically his biological nephew, but his son in every way that mattered—getting him to sleep included. Brax had officially adopted him once he married Tessa, Walker's mom.

"Maci and I are going to the ob-gyn tomorrow. Check on everything." Chance handed out the other two coffees to Luke and Weston.

Brax grinned. "Exciting, terrifying stuff, isn't it?"

"You better believe it."

Weston wasn't paying attention to any of the baby talk. He was zoned in on the footage in front of him. "The stalker has been inactive for too long. Something's not right. He's going to strike soon."

Chance met eyes with Brax, then Luke, behind Weston's back. Weston was definitely the quietest of the four of them, but his intuition was generally spot-on.

If Weston was saying the stalker was going to make another move soon, all of them were willing to believe him.

"I'll get on the phone with LeBlanc and Dorian. Make sure the security around Stella is tight." Luke was already walking out of the conference room, phone in hand.

"She's still in Europe, right?" Brax asked, all traces of tiredness gone.

Chance nodded. "Switzerland, unless they've moved her again." It was possible. Stella didn't like staying too long in one place.

Chance looked over at Weston, who was still studying the footage. "Is there something in particular that has your spidey senses tingling?"

He shook his head without turning from the screen. "No. It's less this footage and more talking to Maci about the guy in the apartment. Do you remember what she told us he said at the apartment?"

"That he knew she wasn't Stella?"

"Actually, the part about battle and honor. That there was honor in staying when Stella had run and hid. It tells us something about his mindset."

Chance rubbed the back of his neck. "That he sees this as some sort of war or competition."

Now Weston turned to look at him. "Yes. All this time we've been searching for the stalker as someone who's obsessed with Stella. And honestly, he may be. But I also think he's obsessed with the *process* of stalking."

Luke came back in the room. "LeBlanc has Stella on lockdown. Guards have eyes on her and will be preparing for a possible attack."

"Did you talk to Dorian?" He had enough experience to understand that sometimes a gut feeling was actionable intel.

"Not directly. He's handling some other business for right now. But I did talk to his second-in-command, and we should be getting a call from Dorian soon to provide any info we can."

"We have reason to believe the stalker might be former military or even law enforcement. Let's run guests at Stella's past events based on that filter and see if we can come up with anything useable."

For the first time they didn't feel like they were looking for a needle in a haystack.

They were maybe thirty minutes in when Chance's phone buzzed. He looked down, expecting a text from

Maci or maybe Dorian. But it was from an unknown number.

Are you particularly attached to your office's front window?

"What the—"

"I just got some sort of weird text about the front window," Brax said. Luke and Weston had gotten it too.

"Sales promotion?" Luke asked.

"From an unknown number?" Brax responded. "Not going to get much business that way."

This wasn't right. All of them knew it. They moved into the office lobby, but the only things there were Maci's empty desk and a few other pieces of furniture.

The window shattered in front of them as a bullet struck it, a sea of glass flying everywhere.

All four of them dove to the ground—Chance behind Maci's desk, Luke and Brax behind a couch, Weston at the corner of the room.

They paused, waiting for another shot to come, but there was nothing but the sound of tinkling glass.

"I have a feeling the stalker just brought the war to us," Luke said.

"Yeah, Weston, why do you have to be so damned right all the time?" Brax backed away from the couch. "How about next time your intuition tells you I'm going to win a million dollars rather than someone shooting at us."

Chance was staring at the chair Maci normally

would've been sitting in. It was covered in glass. Rage was bubbling in his gut. "If Maci had been here…"

"There aren't too many places that someone could have made that shot from," Weston said. "It had to have been from the building across the street."

Chance nodded. "The roof. Let's go. If we move now, maybe we can catch him."

It was an office building with three stories. The shooter would've had a clear range.

Luke was already running toward the weapons room. He yanked out bulletproof vests, throwing them to each of his brothers. They all grabbed their weapons from their desks.

In under a minute they were running out the back door. They all knew this could be a trap, but they weren't going to let that stop them. Not when they had a chance to get the upper hand.

As they rounded the corner from the back alley and had the building across from their office in sight, Chance barked out the plan. "Weston and Brax will clear the top two floors, while Luke and I do the roof. Good?"

His brothers called out their affirmations. They kept their weapons holstered as they ran for the building. It was already pandemonium on the street.

"You think they heard the shot and are panicking?" Luke asked.

As they got closer, the problem became evident. Someone had set off the fire alarm.

He and his brothers looked at each other. "He's giving himself an easy way to escape."

"Split up and look around. Let's see if we can catch anyone acting strange." Weston pulled out his phone and started recording as he walked inside. "I'll try to get as much footage as I can, see if we can match someone to one of Stella's events."

Brax grabbed Chance's arm as someone rushed by, sobbing and yelling about smoke. Maybe the stalker had started an actual fire to make sure there was real panic. "We need to get up on that roof."

Chance shook his head. "There's no way, not with so many people pouring downstairs. Plus, he's already gone. You know he's around here somewhere. Let's record like Weston said."

They spread out, Chance checking every face he passed. He didn't bother looking for a gun bag. The shooter wasn't stupid. He'd either stored the weapon to come back for it later or got out of Dodge immediately after taking the shot.

Chance tried to ignore the most panicked people and the ones who didn't fit the profile. He looked for those who were more calm despite the chaos, and concentrated on recording those.

When the fire engine parked in front of the building and the firefighters began crowd control, Chance knew there was nothing else they could do. They'd talk to local police about the shooting and hopefully get the footage from any security cameras around, but they were limited in what they could do until then. He walked outside as the firefighters demanded it.

Annoyed at the situation, Chance yanked out his

cell with a growl when it rang. Weston. "Please tell me you have good news."

"Unfortunately, nobody walking around with a shirt saying I Just Shot Out a Window. I didn't see anything or anyone who seemed too suspicious," Weston said. "You?"

"A few people who were too relaxed, but nothing concrete."

"Let's get back to the office. We can compare footage and start calling in favors to get the local security feeds. Maybe we caught something."

"I'll meet you there."

A flash of something in his peripheral had him turning, eyes locked with the back of a plain black hoodie. Besides standing slightly taller than the crowd, the man blended in with everyone around him.

Except he was walking away rather than watching what was going on around them.

Chance knew from experience it was human nature to stay at the scene of an emergency. Curiosity and the desire for drama had people sticking around.

Using one hand, he called his brother back.

"I may have something. Man in a black hoodie leaving the scene just to the west of the front door. I'm following."

"We're right behind you."

Chance sped through the crowd, having to jostle to the side as he tried to keep his eyes on the man in the hoodie. At the end of the block the crowd cleared out, and Chance could finally put on some speed. When he was close enough to touch, he reached out and clamped his hand down on the man's shoulder, whirling him around.

Not a man. Another damned teenager. The kid ripped one of his headphones out of his ear with a frown. "Can I help you?"

"Were you in the building back there?" Chance asked.

"No. I stopped by because I heard the sirens, but it doesn't look like there's an actual fire. So I've got better things to do."

Chance still had him by the shoulder of his hoodie. "How do you know there's no fire? People were talking about smoke. Seemed pretty panicked."

The kid shrugged. "Whatever, man. There's no fire."

Chance wanted to push, but knew there was no way in hell this was the stalker. He let the kid go. "You see anything suspicious?"

The kid raised an eyebrow. "You mean besides a random dude grabbing teenagers? No."

Chance fished out a card from his pocket, telling the kid to call if he thought of anything strange. He snapped a picture of the kid's face while he was looking at the card.

They would run him and make sure he didn't have any ties to Stella they should know about. But besides that there wasn't much Chance could do.

He turned and walked back to the office, calling to tell his brothers the hoodie kid was another dead end.

When he got back to the office, he found his brothers hovering around Maci's desk.

"What's going on?"

Luke held up a piece of paper in a gloved hand. "The stalker left us a note."

You made me better, but I want to be the best.
First one to the prize wins.

Chance didn't know what to make of that. "Is the prize Stella?"

Brax dropped his phone to the counter. "I just talked to Dorian, and Stella is safe. No attempts on her."

Chance rubbed his eyes. There were so many things he didn't like about this situation. The stalker actively communicating with them, and coming into their personal space. Him making it into some sort of game he wanted them to play.

But most of all he didn't like the fact that if Maci had been at work today she might have been at that desk when that bastard shot the window out. Might have been covered in glass.

"I need to make a call." He needed to hear Maci's voice.

Chance stepped into his office, dialing before the door was shut.

"Chance? Is everything okay? I was just about to leave so I can work the half day."

Just the sound of Maci's voice—relaxed and calm—soothed his frayed nerves. She was okay. That was all that mattered.

"You're not going to believe this, but we're going to need you to not come in today."

"Damn it, Chance. I am not going to let you—"

"I promise this is not me trying to get you to rest. The front window of the office…broke, and we're going to have to close everything early today and get it fixed."

"Oh, my gosh. Did you throw someone through it?"

He chuckled. "You're not here. So, no."

She laughed at that. "Ha-ha. I've thought about throwing you through that glass once or twice too. What happened?"

"I'll tell you everything when I get home. Do me a favor and make sure the doors are locked."

She didn't respond for a second. "Something happened, didn't it?"

He'd never lied to her and wasn't going to start now. "Yeah. But nobody was hurt."

"Okay," she finally said. He knew she wanted to demand details and appreciated that she didn't. "You all be careful. Come home safe."

Home. To her. "I will. See you in a while."

He walked back out to the main room. Although he hadn't touched it, Luke had found the bullet where it had wedged into the wall. Definitely a downward trajectory. The shooter had been in the building across the street.

"I called some friends on the force," Weston said. "They're going to come pick up the bullet and run it. Brax is on the phone with the window replacement company."

"Maybe we should put in bulletproof glass." Chance meant it as a joke, but Weston's bunched eyebrows said he was really considering it.

Luke stood from where he was studying the bullet. "Good news is that Weston did his voodoo, and because of the special circumstances of our ongoing case, the police have kindly offered to share the security footage from the high-rise to see if we spot anyone we recognize from our own research."

Chance looked over at Weston. He was the one who'd served on the San Antonio PD for a few years. He nodded. "Although, they're more interested in catching the guy who caused the fire panic in the office across the street than they are our window."

Chance shrugged one shoulder. "Since we're almost positive it's the same person, I'll take it."

Luke rubbed his eyes. "Means going through more footage."

It wasn't what any of them wanted to do.

But this bastard had brought the fight to their front door. Chance and his brothers were going to take him down.

Chapter Fifteen

If this was how Chance had felt when he'd found her unconscious in the apartment, then Maci probably needed to cut him some slack.

She was staring at the gaping hole at the front of the office where the wall of glass used to be. Chance had explained what happened last night, but until she saw it with her own eyes this morning, she hadn't truly been able to process it.

It was hard to believe that one bullet had done that much damage. The guys had explained that it had been a rifle bullet, so a big one, but still...*one bullet*.

What if one of the guys had been walking through the lobby, as they did a thousand times a day, when that bullet had hit? Only a little bit of glass had sprayed back far enough to hit her desk—well, hit where her desk *used* to be; the guys had moved it into the conference room where there were no windows—but if Chance had been standing there talking to her when the glass broke, it would have cut him to ribbons.

Now she understood his need to constantly keep her behind him so he was between her and any unknown threats. Because she felt like doing the same thing to him.

She knew if she stayed out watching the workers replacing the window for too long she'd get a lecture from one of the Patterson brothers. As it was, she was only allowed to peek her head around the corner— definitely was *not* allowed to stand in the open room.

But she wasn't going to argue. As long as Chance and his brothers didn't stand in the open room either. Protectiveness went both ways.

The guys were back poring over the new security footage from yesterday. Maci had work she could do at her now-conference-room desk, but could hardly focus. Between the shock of the window and her ob-gyn appointment later that afternoon, she was frazzled.

Her phone buzzed in her pocket and she took it out. Evelyn. Definitely not what she needed today. Maci hadn't answered any of the other five texts since they last saw each other, and planned to ignore this one too.

Maci knew better than to fall for the I miss yous or Let's catch up, babys.

Meet me at your apartment or I'm coming to you.

Maci grit her teeth as she typed back. Today really isn't a good day.

I can either come to that office or your boyfriend's house. Either one. Amazing how quick her mother could be when she wanted to.

Maci rubbed her eyes. She doubted Evelyn had

Chance's address, but it wouldn't be impossible. Maci didn't want her showing up at either place.

Especially not today when she and Chance were going together to the doctor. Maci didn't want to produce proof in living color of the poor genes their child would be getting from Maci's side of the family.

Not to mention the questions it might lead to about Maci's mothering ability. *Legitimate* questions.

Ones she'd asked herself every single day since she found out she was pregnant.

Fine. I'll be at my place in twenty.

She headed into the conference room. The guys were so closely watching the footage, none of them even realized she was there. She walked over to Chance.

"I'm going to go and rest for a little while before the doctor's appointment."

Chance was on his feet immediately. "Are you okay? Do you feel sick? I can drive you home."

They'd ridden in together. She'd forgotten about that. "No, no. You have important and time-sensitive work to be done. I'm okay to drive myself."

He was torn, she could tell. She hated that she was deceiving him, but what choice did she have?

She reached out and touched his arm. "No smothering, remember? You can walk me out to the car, and I'll text you when I…get there."

That was vague enough not to be a complete lie.

He still didn't like it, but agreed. "Okay, I'll walk you out." He wrapped an arm around her shoulder and led her to the back alley, where they'd all parked today to avoid the front door.

He pulled her in for a hug at the car. She hugged him back. She needed his closeness.

"Be careful," he said into her hair. "And let me know you're okay. I'll see you at home."

Guilt ate at Maci. Chance wanted her to be safe and she was running off to meet with an unstable woman, but if she could spare him another run-in with her mother, she would. With a wave to Chance, she got in the car and headed back to the past.

MACI'S MOTHER WAS pacing in front of the door when she arrived.

"Took you long enough."

Maci ignored her, quickly texting Chance that she was okay, before ushering them both inside. The sooner she took care of this, the sooner she could get back to the better parts of her life.

"What do you want, Mom?"

As if she didn't know. As if calling Evelyn *Mom* wasn't practically a joke.

"You could at least pretend to be happy to see me." Evelyn walked around looking at things in the apartment like she'd never seen them before and was fascinated by how Maci had decorated. "I don't even know what's going on with you. You rushed me out of here so fast last time."

Maci grit her teeth. She knew how this game was played. Evelyn was going to do whatever was the exact opposite of what Maci wanted.

If Maci wanted to spend time and try to connect, Evelyn would want to leave. If Maci was on a tight schedule, Evelyn would be clingy and refuse to leave.

It was a childish game, and they'd been playing it for as long as Maci could remember—even when she lived at home.

"I need cash."

Of course, she did. "What happened to what I just gave you the other day? You can't have run through it all already."

"You didn't give me that much."

"Because I don't have much to spare. Any, actually."

Evelyn spun around to stare at her, crossing her thin arms over her chest. "We both know that's not true. I saw the car your boyfriend was driving when he took you out of here. I know he owns his own company with those so-called brothers of his. I don't believe they all aren't loaded."

Maci hated hearing her even mentioning Chance or his brothers. The Pattersons were all good. Chance deserved better than to be dragged into Maci's toxic family drama.

"First of all, he's not my boyfriend. And yes, I may work for the Pattersons, who own their own business, but that doesn't mean they're loaded and it especially doesn't mean I have extra money."

Evelyn started walking around again. "But you could get it if you wanted to. Especially to help out family."

Maci sat down in the kitchen chair by the small table. This pattern with her mother was never going to end. Not if Maci continued to let it go on like this.

"Mom, I don't have money to give you. I need it for myself."

Her mother turned to scrutinize her. "I thought you were done with drugs."

"I am." She took in a deep breath, hoping she wasn't about to make a huge mistake. "I need the money because I'm going to have a baby."

Maci's pregnancy was too new for her to have thought much about how she would break the news to Evelyn. But sitting here, she realized that she hoped the news would bring about some sort of positive change.

Evelyn had never been able to clean up for Maci, but maybe she would for her grandchild. Maybe they could have a relationship after all.

Her mother stopped and stared at her. "You idiot. You let him get you pregnant? You've ruined your life."

Knots formed in Maci's stomach. Definitely not the reaction she'd been hoping for.

"Thanks for the vote of confidence. Regardless of my *poor decisions* I don't have the money, so go find someone else to extort."

Evelyn was silent, turning back and walking around the room, peeking at all of Maci's things. Every time she picked something up, Maci ached to reach out and slap her hands away. This was her space, her sanctuary, and she wanted Evelyn out of it.

"You think I'm stupid?" Evelyn picked up a book and tossed it on the couch. "I know you have a rainy-day fund. I'll take that. You can ask your baby daddy for more money for raising some thankless brat."

"You should leave, Evelyn. I've made my decision."

Evelyn's eyes were flinty. She didn't like when Maci called her by her name instead of Mom. As if Evelyn hadn't just described her as a thankless brat.

"You've made your decision?" She picked up another book, flipping through the pages before tossing it to the side. "Do you think you're better than me?"

"This isn't about better or worse. This is about priorities."

"Oh, yeah?" She put her hands on her hips. "How do you think your little boyfriend would react if he knew what you used to do to get high? Don't you think someone should explain that to him so he knows what he's getting into?"

Dread pooled in Maci's stomach as she steeled herself against the memories. She refused to go back to that time, even in her mind. "I made mistakes. He would accept them, especially since I won't make them again."

Maybe if she said the words forcefully enough she could believe they were true.

Her mother laughed, a harsh bark of a sound. "I doubt that. He seems like an upstanding guy. A professional and respectable businessman."

"He is."

Evelyn's lip curled up in a snarl. "Men like that have one thought when it comes to drugs—once addicted, always addicted."

No. Maci wasn't addicted anymore. She was in recovery. She'd done everything she could to get better. She *was* better.

"I'm not like you. I'm not going to keep doing drugs when I've finally made a life for myself. I'm not going to spend forever chasing a high I'll never be able to keep. I'm happy sober."

It was the wrong thing to say and it threw Evelyn into a rage. Maci stood there in horror as Evelyn swept out the rest of Maci's books off the bookshelf and onto the floor, then knocked the bookshelf over. The coffee table ended up on its side, with the empty glass that had been sitting on it shattering on the floor. Evelyn tore pillows and ripped the paintings and pictures from the walls.

It was impossible to believe someone as petite as Evelyn could do this much damage—the drugs in her system gave her the boost of strength. Maci knew not to get near. Evelyn didn't have these rages often, but her violence wasn't just targeted on inanimate objects. Maci kept far out of reach.

By the time Evelyn was done, the apartment that Maci had fought and scrounged for was nothing but scraps and trash.

"You ungrateful little bitch." Maci watched her mother's chest heave with every angry breath. "You either get me my money or we'll see what your boyfriend says when he finds out his baby mama was a drug dealer and a whore."

There it was, Evelyn's trump card. There was nothing else to do. Maci knew it and so did Evelyn. Her smarmy grin was enough to prove it.

"Fine. Let's go find an ATM."

Twenty minutes later, Maci's bank account was empty—including the five hundred dollars she'd saved for emergencies.

And so was her heart. She felt hollowed out as she watched her mother slip away laughing, leaving her alone with her thoughts.

Now that Evelyn had a button to push, Maci would never be free. She'd lose everything she'd worked so hard for and Chance… Chance would eventually find out what Maci had done. The first time she tried to refuse Evelyn, she'd tell him everything and he'd hate Maci for it. It was only a matter of time.

Maci didn't know what to do with herself but she couldn't move yet, so she curled up on her couch and cried, as the future she'd been so desperate for slipped from her fingers for good.

Chapter Sixteen

Something wasn't right.

Chance told himself not to read into Maci's stiffness and slightly weird pauses as he walked her out to the car, but he couldn't help it.

Certainly, there were a lot of things for her to be stressed over...the window, the doctor's appointment, her head wound, the stalker in general. But something hadn't been right about how she'd left.

He'd still let her go and still forced himself to come back into the office once she was gone. He'd felt slightly better when he'd received her text—Made it okay—but something still didn't sit right in his gut.

He made it another hour before he decided to stop fighting it. "I'm going to go. Maci and I have that doctor's appointment this afternoon and... I don't know."

"You alright?" Weston looked up from his screen.

"Yeah. I just want to make sure she's okay."

None of them argued. Luke just tossed Chance his keys since Maci had taken Chance's car.

But when he got home neither his car nor Maci was there. Normally stepping inside the house—especially since Maci had been staying there—made him relax, but not this time. Everything was silent.

Hoping there was some reason she was here despite the car not being in the garage, he called for her. "Maci?"

Pulling out his phone, he dialed her number and was immediately sent to voice mail. He sent texts, but got no response and no indication they'd been received.

He checked everywhere. The bedrooms were empty, the living room was clear and so was the backyard. There was no sign of trouble or forced entry. Every window was closed, every door locked.

Everything was exactly how it should have been, just without Maci.

Chance tried to focus. There hadn't been any other signs of attack. Nothing was out of place, no blood anywhere. Plus, no one except his family knew that Maci had been living with him.

So, she probably hadn't been kidnapped. Had there been a car accident?

No, because she'd texted him that she'd arrived safely.

He froze in the process of looking around again. Maybe she'd left? Like the night she'd snuck out of his bed and never returned. Maybe she'd decided she didn't want to be here with him anymore.

Maybe she'd decided to cut him out of her and the baby's life completely.

He rushed to the closet, heaving a sigh of relief when her clothes were still there.

He was about to dial his brothers to start a search

party when he heard the garage door open. Relief warred with frustration so acute he had to take deep breaths to keep from losing his cool.

How he acted now was important. Because ultimately Maci was a grown woman and she didn't have to report any of her actions to him. He needed to show her that he was concerned but not smothering.

She walked in the door and his eyes combed over her—no injuries; that was good.

"Where the hell were you?" he barked.

Great, Patterson. Nice and calm.

She stilled on her way past, eyes narrowing. "I was driving around."

She looked tired, pale. Why?

"You were supposed to come straight home. Do you have any idea how—"

"I needed some time to think, Chance. Give me a break."

He could feel frustration bubbling up inside him. "You promised you'd come straight home and let me know you were okay. When I got your text, I assumed that's what it meant."

She flinched. "I had something to do first."

"Which was?"

Maci's hands clenched at her sides. "Nothing that concerns you."

"Everything about you concerns me."

"Well, it shouldn't! I'm a grown woman, Chance. I can take care of myself for a few hours."

Chance deflated. He was messing up…again. Letting fear drive him. If he wasn't careful, he knew he'd drive them apart.

He took a deep breath and tried again. "I know you can take care of yourself. I was worried. I came home and you weren't here and I couldn't get ahold of you. We have an active stalker who's targeting San Antonio Security, so now is a bad time to go AWOL without anyone knowing where. That's true for all of us."

Maci's eyes closed and she sighed. Chance watched the defensiveness in her posture slowly disappear. For a long moment they stood there in silence, then she came over and slid her arms around him.

The knot in his chest finally loosened as he clutched her tight. She was okay. She wasn't hurt and she hadn't left him.

When she spoke it was hushed. Apologetic. "I'm sorry. I wasn't even thinking about all that. I thought I would make it home before you. I didn't mean to make you worry."

He stroked her hair, brushing it off her face so he could see it better where it rested on his chest. "I'm sorry that I snapped at you. Are you okay? You look pretty stressed. Is it office stuff? The window?"

He couldn't blame her if she didn't feel safe there anymore.

"No. I can't stand the thought of you guys getting hurt, but that isn't it. I was at my place with my mother."

He wanted to ask why being with her mom made her look so defeated and bone weary. But he wanted her to tell him because she wanted to tell him, not because he was prying. "Can I do anything for you?"

"This is good. I think I needed it."

He wrapped her up tighter, nuzzling his cheek against her hair. "So did I."

"It's almost time to get ready for the doctor's appointment," she murmured. "They're going to tell us the gender. Are you nervous?"

"No, not nervous. Are you hoping for a boy or a girl?"

"Maybe a handsome little boy like his father."

He grinned. "I think I'd like to have a little hellion of a daughter. She'd be the spitting image of her mama."

Maci stiffened against him for a moment, then relaxed. "Two Maci Fords in the world is probably one too many."

Chance wasn't sure what that meant, so he let it go. It sounded like a cliché, but boy or girl didn't matter to him. He just wanted both mother and child healthy.

MACI AND CHANCE sat in silence a few hours later in the ob-gyn's waiting room. She was feeling more nervous every minute.

When her name was finally called, Chance stuck by her side. He helped her into the gown and moved one of the chairs right next to the exam table. Although she didn't like to be fussed over, Maci couldn't help but admit it was nice to not be alone.

A nurse came in and did some medical basics, then the ultrasound tech entered, all smiles. For some reason that made Maci even more nervous.

"Have you seen the baby yet?" the tech asked. Both Maci and Chance shook their heads and she smiled. "You're in for a treat."

With a squirt of cool gel and a wiggle of the ultra-sound wand, a whooshing sound filled Maci's ears.

"That hummingbird-like sound is the heartbeat," the tech explained.

Maci felt the pinprick of tears at the back of her lids. That was her baby's heartbeat. Chance's baby. As if she'd called to him, he reached for her hand, squeezing her fingers lightly. She looked up and saw the faintest sheen of moisture in his eyes too.

They watched the wiggling bean on the screen until it was over, and the tech handed them page after page of sonograms. The tech explained that the doctor would answer all their questions, including the gender if they wanted to know, and then left with as big a smile as she'd had when she came in.

"Alright, Ms. Ford. It seems like you're doing great!" Dr. Harris was also full of smiles when he entered. "You and baby both look healthy."

"So, the all-day puking she has sometimes is normal?" Chance asked.

Dr. Harris laughed and kept his eyes on Maci. "Yep. Morning sickness is a terrible name considering it has no internal clock, but it's completely normal. You haven't lost a lot of weight, so I'm not worried about it. Just keep doing what you can to take care of yourself. That part should be over soon."

"Thank goodness." Maci grinned. "I won't miss it at all."

Dr. Harris continued to go over test results from both today and ones that had been run at the hospital. He reassured Maci and Chance that the baby was fine.

No damage had come from the attack, and there didn't seem to be any genetic issues either.

"You elected to get an early gender test. We have the results if you still want to know."

Maci looked at Chance. He shrugged. "Your choice. I'm good either way."

She looked back at the doctor. She wanted to know. "Tell us."

Dr. Harris smiled. "Congratulations. You're having a girl."

A girl. They were having a daughter. Maci couldn't pull her focus from that thought.

She was bringing a new Ford woman into the world.

The rest of the appointment felt like it moved at lightning speed, with Maci only partially aware of it. Dr. Harris provided suggestions concerning exercise and foods that might help settle her stomach. He answered all the questions Chance had while Maci sat there feeling numb. By the time she refocused on the world around her, Chance was bundling her into the car.

He slid into his seat and just sat there, keys in hand while he stared out the windshield. "We're having a baby. A girl. *Our* girl."

There was awe and adoration in Chance's voice. When she glanced over, his eyes practically twinkled with joy. His smile was about to split his face.

So why did Maci feel the heavy weight of despair in her stomach?

A *girl*. She felt stuck on the knowledge that she and Chance were having a daughter. What did Maci know about raising a daughter when Evelyn was supposed to be her example?

Evelyn had been so deep in her own drug addiction, in and out of court-required rehab, that she didn't have the ability to protect Maci from anything. Then Maci had followed in her footsteps without a care. She'd found peace at the bottom of a pill bottle or heavier drugs.

It didn't matter that Maci had cleaned herself up, that she'd been sober for years. She was still always only one bad choice away from being back in that pit.

What kind of person brought a baby into the world to have a mother with addiction?

She put her hands on her stomach. Her baby was just one more cog in the chain of messed up Ford women. Maci didn't know how to break the cycle. She didn't know how to raise her daughter right. She didn't know anything about boundaries or parenting. She didn't know how she'd keep her child safe.

Her daughter was going to pay the price for Maci's stupidity. The thought made Maci sick.

She'd ruined her baby's life before she'd even got a chance to live it.

As they neared Chance's house, panic forced her breaths to come faster. The second he parked, she shot out of the car—she was going to be sick and it had nothing to do with morning sickness.

She couldn't be near him, couldn't speak to him. She'd ruined it all.

"Maci?" Chance grabbed her arm to reel her into his body, but she yanked it away.

"I'm going to go to bed."

"What about dinner? You need to eat."

The idea of sitting down and facing Chance made Maci's stomach clench even worse. "I'm not hungry."

She could feel Chance's eyes on her the whole way into the house, but she didn't turn back. She couldn't. Not when she'd ruined his life and he didn't even know it.

Chapter Seventeen

Chance barely slept a wink. All night long, his thoughts drifted to Maci. He couldn't stop picturing her after the appointment. The hunch of her shoulders as she bolted into the house, the stiff set of her lip as she tried not to cry.

Was it the baby? Did she not want a girl? Even if that was the case, he couldn't see Maci getting that upset over something like gender. It was something else, he knew it, but he had no idea how to find out. Maci had locked herself in the guest bedroom, refusing to come out for dinner, even when he'd asked as gently as possible. He'd almost decided to break down the door and demand to know what was going on.

Then he heard Maci crying.

Even through the door, Chance could tell that her tears were agonized. It wasn't just the typical fear of being a bad parent, she was terrified about something else, and that took the wind out of his sails. As frustrated as he was, Chance refused to badger her when she was obviously going through something difficult.

Worst of all, it was a reminder that, as much as he

cared for her, he didn't know a lot about Maci. So, as much as he wanted to demand answers, he stepped away and let her be.

It was the hardest thing he'd ever done.

By the time he'd gotten up this morning, the kitchen showed signs of Maci having made herself tea and breakfast. That was good. He wanted her to talk to him, but if she wouldn't, at least she was taking care of herself.

He'd barely made his own coffee and breakfast when his phone rang.

"We got another message from the stalker," Brax said.

A sliver of unease dug into Chance. He didn't like the way Brax's voice sounded—too careful and controlled for his free-spirited jokester of a brother.

"What did it say?"

"I think you should come in and see for yourself."

Chance didn't even have to think about it. "I can't. I need to stay here with Maci."

That got Brax's attention. He cursed under his breath. "I forgot about the appointment yesterday. Is everything okay with the baby?"

"The baby's good." Chance was careful not to let the gender slip. He wasn't sure if Maci wanted people to know yet. "Maci's just having a…tough time."

Brax was quiet for too long, and the foreboding got stronger.

"What's going on, Brax?"

"The message was a threat."

"Did you guys already let Dorian know? Is Stella secure?"

"It wasn't a threat against Stella."

Chance let out a curse. "Against us again?"

Brax didn't answer.

"What the hell is going on?" Brax was never this quiet.

A second later he heard a click. "Bro, it's Weston. Luke's on too. You and Maci both okay?"

This definitely wasn't good. "Yeah, we're fine. You guys need to tell me what's going on right damned now."

"The new threat is against Maci," Weston said quietly.

The world stopped. "What kind of threat?"

"I sent a picture to your email."

Chance reached for the computer, fingers slamming down on the keys as he found the picture of the letter Weston had sent. Curses flew out of his mouth as he read, fury burning through him with every word.

It's a pity when the innocent get caught in the cross fire of battle, don't you think?

But war is what this is and I'm determined to win.

With your queen as a prize, I'll do whatever it takes to defeat you. I'm looking forward to it.

You make me good, but she will make me better.

Included with the letter was a picture of Maci coming out of the office. It was impossible to tell how long ago it had been taken.

Every nerve in Chance's body demanded action. He wanted to move.

He wanted to *kill*.

Whoever this bastard was who wanted to drag Maci into his sick games… Chance wanted to erase him from the planet.

"Hang on," he said into the phone, before tossing it onto the kitchen table. He was tempted to throw his laptop across the room in rage, but knew in the long run that would only hinder his ability to protect Maci.

Right now he needed to see with his own eyes that she was alright. Especially after last night's disappearing act.

He knocked on the guest bedroom door. "Maci? I just need to know that you're in there and you're okay."

To his surprise, she opened the door. She looked pale and a little fragile, but otherwise fine.

Before he could stop himself, he yanked her into his arms.

"Chance?" she whispered.

"We've got trouble," he said, not letting her go. He wasn't going to keep this from her. He respected her too much not to tell her if she was in danger. "A threat from the stalker directed at you. I'm on the phone with the guys."

Her face got paler, but she nodded. He led her back out to the kitchen and grabbed his phone as she sat down in one of the chairs, pulling her knees up and wrapping her arms around them.

She looked so young and vulnerable. Her personality was so big, it was easy to forget that Maci was only in her early twenties.

He put his phone on speaker mode. "I'm back. Maci's here with me."

"Hi, sweetheart," Brax said. "We're so sorry about this."

"I'm okay," she said. "Let's treat this like it was any other case. Try to keep our emotions out of it."

The hell he could. But Chance just nodded. He spun the laptop in her direction so she could see the note.

"Where was the letter sent?"

"The office," Luke said. "It might have been there a day or more, honestly. Mail hasn't been a priority."

"Guy is talking about war and battle," Weston said. "I think we were on the right track when we were narrowing the list to people who are former military or law enforcement."

"I don't understand what's made him change from Stella to me." Maci's voice was small.

Chance reached over and grabbed her hand, rubbing his thumb along her soft skin. "We think this has never necessarily been about Stella. Stalking is a game for this guy."

"Probably closer is that he considers it to be an exercise or a military mission," Weston interjected. "He's trying to improve his skills and feels like going up against us will help do that."

"So, targeting one of our own makes sure we're willing to engage with him," Luke said. "If he stuck with Stella, he has no guarantee we won't quit or get fired."

She shook her head. "Did I do something to make him come after me?"

Chance squeezed her hand. "No, honey. He thrives on a challenge. That's what all of us are to him."

But Chance damn well wished they'd never put Maci

undercover to begin with. Then this bastard would've never known she existed.

"You and Maci need to get somewhere safe until we can figure this out," Brax said. "Definitely can't bring her to the office or let her be at her apartment alone. Hell, I wouldn't even stay at your house."

"I'll take her to Mom and Dad's."

Luke snorted. "Finally, it's your turn."

Chance's mouth twitched into a small smile. It did seem like Sheila and Clinton's home had turned into an unofficial safe house over the past couple of years. All three of Chance's brothers had brought their women there at one point or another.

"I'll get Maci settled, then be back."

The brothers went over a few more details before Chance got off the phone. A quick call to his mother and everything was ready to go.

Maci was still sitting with her arms wrapped around her legs.

He brushed a strand of hair back from her face. "You okay? We should pack and get ready to go."

"I don't want your parents to get hurt. I know they watch Walker too."

"We'll leave if anything gets dicey for them, I promise." It was an easy promise for Chance to make. He didn't want his family getting hurt either.

"Does…" She trailed off and started again. "Do your parents know about the baby?"

"I doubt it. I know the guys know, but they wouldn't tell, and I didn't want to just drop it on them via text or something."

"Oh. Okay."

"We can keep it hushed for now if you want."

She nodded. "That would probably be best."

He wasn't sure exactly what that meant. He still wasn't sure why she'd been so upset last night.

Had she changed her mind about keeping the baby? The thought crushed something inside him, but now wasn't the time to get into it.

They packed up and twenty minutes later were on the road. Neither of them spoke much and the silence strained between them. He wanted to say something to make things easier for her but had no idea what to say.

The last thing he wanted to do was share Maci with anyone, even his parents. He wanted to sit her down and talk, to get everything out in the open—especially after yesterday's appointment and breakdown. But her safety had to come first. They'd have plenty of chances to talk about her past when the time was right.

Right now, Maci's past didn't matter. What mattered was keeping her safe from this stalker.

Chapter Eighteen

Maci felt like her life was falling apart on every possible level.

She was still reeling from yesterday's panic attack, then discovered she was the target of a stalker, and now had to stay with her not-boyfriend's parents who didn't know she was having his baby.

She wasn't sure which terrified her most.

Sheila and Clinton Patterson had always been kind to her. They'd often invited her over for holiday dinners and brought coffee for her on the rare occasion that they stopped into the office to visit their sons. They were good people.

But being nice to Maci as one of San Antonio Security's employees was much different than accepting her as the mother of Chance's child.

This was definitely something she'd need to keep hidden.

"You planning to stay in the car until you blend into the seats?"

Maci startled at Chance's voice. She'd been so stuck

in her thoughts that she hadn't noticed him park. He stood next to her open door, waiting.

He held out his hand to help her out. "You ready?"

Not even remotely. But she nodded and got out of the car. At the door, Sheila Patterson stood with a smile on her face and her arms open wide. Even from feet away, Maci could see how much love she had for Chance.

She had that much love for all of her family.

"Chance, honey, good to have you home. Maci, welcome. You're looking well." Sheila wrapped them each in quick hugs before grinning. "There's someone here to see you both."

Chance smiled at his mom and took off for the living room, scooping the young boy from the carpet. Walker, Brax and Tessa's son, was babbling his uncle's ear off in unintelligible toddler language, but Chance didn't seem to mind. He gave the boy his full attention, nodding and adding to the conversation as much as he could.

Maci's heart turned to mush. What an amazing father Chance was going to be. She wished she could say the same about being a mother.

Walker continued to coo as Chance handed him over to Clinton. "Thank you for letting us stay for a while. We just need to get off-grid."

Sheila smiled. "At this point we're used to it. And you boys know this is your home too. You're always welcome. You can stay in your room, and I've made up the guest room for Maci."

"I have to get back to the office. There are some things that need to be handled immediately, but I'll be back later." He kissed his mother's cheek and waved at his dad, who was getting an earful from Walker.

Then to Maci's surprise, he wrapped her in a hug, pressing a kiss to her temple. "Get some rest."

Well, it was obvious she wasn't just an employee anymore.

The tension felt thick, despite baby Walker's jabbering and giggling as Maci stood there with Sheila and Clinton.

"Why don't I show you up to the room where you'll be staying?"

Maci grabbed her small bag and followed Sheila. She showed Maci to a simple guest room, and Maci dropped off her stuff. The bed wasn't very big, but it looked inviting. She wished she could crawl into it and pull the covers over her head.

"Bathroom is just down the hall." Sheila turned and smiled as she opened a door to another bedroom. "And lest you think I'm completely old-fashioned or disapprove of you in any way, this is Chance's room."

Maci had to smile as she saw the twin bed and small desk. Sports posters all over the wall. There definitely wasn't room for a second person. "Oh."

"I know, I should redecorate. But I haven't touched any of the boys' rooms. They came in and made the space their own. For all of them it was the first bedroom that was truly only theirs."

"That's wonderful."

Sheila shrugged and led her back downstairs. "I guess these rooms are a reminder that sometimes families are formed in nontraditional ways, but that doesn't make them any less of a family."

Families definitely weren't Maci's area of expertise.

Sheila walked back downstairs, blowing kisses at Clinton and Walker still playing in the living room before leading Maci into the kitchen. "It's been a stressful day for you. How about some coffee? The boys got me one of the fancy espresso machines for Christmas last year. You like cappuccinos, right?"

"I, uh, I switched over to tea recently."

Shelia spun to look at her. "You're pregnant."

Maci wasn't sure what to say. "You got that from tea?"

"More that I knew the boys weren't telling us something. I thought maybe it had to do with a case. But Chance's protective hug clarified it all for me." She smiled gently. "Although it was the tea that clinched it. You love cappuccinos."

"I do miss cappuccinos." Maci chose a tea bag from the tin Sheila held out. "Are you mad?"

"Why would I be mad?"

Maci shrugged. "I don't think anyone in the family even knew Chance and I were…together. Maybe you think I'm trying to trap him or something."

It's what Evelyn had done to Maci's father… Gotten pregnant to force him to marry her.

Sheila gave a little laugh. "Honey, have you met Chance? Nobody forces him to do anything he doesn't want to do."

She relaxed and let out a little laugh herself. "Yeah. That's pretty true."

"We already considered you part of this family. You and that baby are Pattersons, and we'll have your back no matter what. Even if it doesn't work out between you and Chance."

"That means a lot to me."

They fell into a comfortable silence as Maci sipped her tea and they listened to Walker and Clinton play. She thought of Chance's interaction with his nephew.

"Chance will be such a good dad," Maci whispered.

"You'll both be great parents."

"I'm not so sure about me."

"I am." Sheila reached over and patted her hand. "Parenthood is more about instincts than anything else. I've seen you with Walker and you're great with him. I'm not worried one bit."

Sheila thought she knew Maci, but she really didn't. Maci frowned into her cup until a hand on her shoulder lifted her gaze again.

"I know my son. He's been enamored with you since the day you met. All the fighting? Everybody knew that was you and Chance's way of flirting with each other. Like kids on a playground."

Maci gave a half smile. "Yeah, we definitely have a tug-on-the-pigtails vibe."

"There for a bit a few months ago, Chance was happier. Smiling more and laughing. Then it was gone."

Because Maci had come to her senses and left him sleeping in his own bed. She didn't want to explain any of this to Sheila.

When Maci didn't say anything, Sheila eventually

nodded and leaned back. "Regardless of what happened, I think you two can make it work."

"I don't," Maci blurted. She was not in line to be the next Mrs. Patterson. Chance needed someone better. "I wish we could, but regardless of everything that's happened, there's a lot he doesn't know about me. I'm not who he needs."

"I'm not so sure that's your choice, but if there are things he needs to know, tell him."

"You say it like it's easy."

"I don't mean to," Sheila admitted. "Baring your soul to someone you care about is the hardest thing you can do, but I will say that it's usually worth the pain. My son isn't a weak man. He's not going to run at the first sign of trouble with you. He hasn't yet, has he?"

No, he hadn't. Chance had been right there at Maci's side every day. He'd given her space when she needed it, yet still pushed her to talk to him whenever he could. He wanted answers, but he hadn't been cruel or malicious.

He'd been gentle. Not a word anyone would normally associate with Chance.

As if she heard Maci's thoughts running wild, Sheila grabbed her hand and smiled. "Chance is a born caretaker. It's how he shows his love. Trust him to take care of you and the baby. He's always going to do right by his family, and you can be the heart of that if you just tell him what you need and what scares you most."

Maci bit her lip, processing the words.

"Trust that what's in his heart for you is enough to keep him at your side," Sheila continued. "It may not be easy to fight your natural skepticism, but the battle will be worth it. I promise."

Maci had nothing to say to that, but Sheila didn't seem to need her words. This woman seemed to understand more about Maci than her own mother ever had.

Emotion urged Maci forward and she drew Sheila into a hug. "Thank you."

"There's nothing to thank me for." She ran a hand down Maci's hair, and for a moment, she knew exactly what a mother's love felt like. It was beautiful.

"Now, give me your cup and go take a nap," Sheila said with a playful smile and nudge toward the stairs. "Growing my grandbaby is hard—but very important—work."

Feeling lighter than she had in ages, Maci went upstairs to rest.

Chapter Nineteen

Chance could feel exhaustion weighing him down by the time he got back to his parents' house. It was well after midnight, so everyone was already in bed. Dad had kept him updated via text throughout the day just to reassure him everything was okay on the home front.

He was glad stuff was okay somewhere, because it surely hadn't been in the office.

Weston had called in every favor he had left with the San Antonio PD to get a rushed lab report on the stalker's letter, only for the report to come back with nothing. The letter was completely clean—not a single fingerprint or hair, nothing that could give them a clue. Even the stamp hadn't been licked.

It was a complete dead end.

They'd pored over more footage. Ran faces and names through every program they had available to them. Dorian and his team had shown up to help too. Just because the stalker seemed to have moved on to Maci didn't necessarily mean Stella was safe.

They all wanted to catch this bastard.

But he was still one step ahead of them, because once again, all their work had amounted to nothing.

Everyone had finally decided to call it a night. His brothers went home to the women who loved them. Chance went home to the woman who seemed only a half breath away from taking off in a dead sprint.

Chance scrubbed a hand over his face as he sat down in the kitchen. He didn't know how to help Maci with whatever was going on in her mind any more than he knew how to stop this stalker.

Uselessness wasn't a feeling he was accustomed to or liked.

Chance sat on a stool in the dark kitchen and thought about the past twenty-four hours. The doctor's appointment, Maci's silence, the note—he wasn't sure the best way to handle any of it. He wanted to wrap Maci in bubble wrap, to insulate her and their daughter from the world, but that wasn't his call.

Their *daughter*.

When they heard her heartbeat for the first time, he'd been overwhelmed by emotion. He could already see a little girl with Maci's nose and his eyes. He was ecstatic.

The baby and Maci were every dream he'd never let himself have. He had no recollection of his own biological parents. And while he would lay the world at the feet of Sheila and Clinton, this baby would be the only biological relation Chance had ever really known.

But where he was full of joy, Maci was shutting down and shutting him out. Running. *Again.*

Why did she always run?

Even after all the passion between them. Even when they could hardly be in the same room with each other without touching one another—magnets drawn together in a way they couldn't resist.

But still Maci refused to truly get close to him.

Chance wasn't surprised when he heard his mother's soft footsteps come down the stairs. Had he ever sat in this kitchen having a crisis without Mom somehow knowing and making her way here?

"Hey, Mom." He stood to put some water on for tea. Maybe something warm with no caffeine would help him settle down.

"Hey, baby. You just getting home? Long hours for you."

"I've been home for a little while, but yeah, long hours."

"You've got a lot on your mind. And not just what's going on with this case. I had a talk with Maci today."

"You know about the baby." He gave her a shrug and a smile. "I'm surprised she told you. But I shouldn't be, I guess."

"It was more that I put the pieces together than she actually told me, but yeah. Congratulations."

She wrapped her arms around him and he let himself sink into his mother's hug. Sheila Patterson had always been his safe space. From the moment he'd finally stopped fighting them, his parents had become his rocks, grounding and centering him when nothing else could. They'd earned his trust over and over again.

It was what he wanted to be for Maci, if she'd let him.

They finally broke apart when the kettle whistled. Sheila moved to put tea bags in the mugs.

"We found out we're having a girl yesterday."

"You excited about that?"

"I didn't care either way, but yeah. To think about a little Maci running around, that makes my heart happy."

He thought of Maci's reaction and his smile faded.

"But?" Sheila prompted.

"Maci seemed fine and then she just shut down. I'm talking practically catatonic. She hid in the bedroom as soon as we got home."

He stood, pacing the length of the kitchen as he tried to work out his thoughts. "I always seem to mess up with her, Mom. She runs away, and I don't know how to make her understand I would do anything for her and the baby."

His mom was silent as she watched him move, sipping her drink with that calmness that made it so easy to share his feelings. Finally, she set the cup down and folded her hands.

"You've been taking care of others since before you could take care of yourself. It's your first instinct with the people who are important to you."

Chance frowned. "Yeah."

"I know you've been taking care of Maci, that's what you do. But when's the last time you listened to her or even asked what she wanted? Do you even know if she wants to be a mother?"

Panic seared through Chance. He wanted his baby, but he wanted her with Maci. He wanted them to be a family. The idea that Maci might not want it too was almost too much to take.

His mom reached out and grabbed his hand. "Do you want to know what I see when I look at Maci? I see someone who's scared."

Chance shook his head. "Maci's the strongest person I know. She's not scared of anything."

But there was something in the back of his mind that was screaming at him, that maybe his mother was right.

Sheila shrugged. "That could be exactly what she wants people to think. I think maybe her past is haunting her, and with a baby representing such an important future, it's scary for her."

He rubbed his eyes. "Why doesn't she just tell me this?"

"I think our Maci's been alone for a long time. She might not know how to."

She didn't know how to say what she needed to say, so she ran instead. Put walls up.

"There's nothing she could tell me about her past that's going to change how I feel about her."

His mother smiled gently. "In this house, we've always believed in second chances. We've always believed that the past didn't dictate the future. I think you're going to have to introduce her to those concepts."

"Yeah, I think you're right."

"I'm going back to bed. I hope you'll get some sleep too." She stood up. "And, Chance, when you talk to Maci, really listen to her. Take off your I'll-fix-everything hat, and just really listen. I think that's what she needs most of all."

JUST AFTER DAWN, Chance woke, rubbing grit out of his eyes as he stumbled into the kitchen. He'd gone to bed right after his talk with his mother and gotten a few hours of sleep, but what she'd said still kept playing in his mind.

He needed to listen to Maci. Not do. Not fix. *Listen.*

He found a note from his mother on the counter.

Dad and I are out for the day. Be home by dinner. Make your girl some breakfast and talk. Love, Mom

Chance hunted down the pots, pans and food he'd need to make a great pancake breakfast, something he knew how to do, since he and his brothers had been in charge of breakfast on the weekends. Maci shuffled into the kitchen just as he was finishing.

"Perfect timing," he said with a smile.

She stopped in the doorway. "I thought you would be Sheila."

"Mom and Dad went out for the day, but I was instructed to make you breakfast. I made pancakes, home fries, toast and even some eggs if your stomach is up for them. There's some cut fruit in the fridge too."

"Wow. That's quite the spread. What's the occasion?"

Chance shrugged. "You need to eat and we need to talk. Might as well kill two birds."

"Talk?"

"Talk," Chance said firmly. "Well, you need to talk and I need to listen."

She sat down at the kitchen island, and he pushed some food toward her to get her to eat. She took each bite slowly, as if each mouthful brought her closer to a firing squad.

He sat down next to her with his own plate. "Before we start, I wanted to say I'm sorry."

She looked over at him, still chewing. "What do you have to be sorry for?"

"This whole time, I've been more concerned about myself and my feelings than yours. I didn't even ask the most basic question."

"Which is?"

"Do you want to be a mom?"

"You did ask me. You asked me in the hospital if I was keeping the baby."

He nodded. "I know. But that's not the same thing. What I'm asking you now is if you *want* to be a mom."

She swallowed, setting her fork down. "I do, but…" She trailed off to silence.

"But what? Whatever it is, speak it."

"My mom is pretty unstable. She was addicted—*is* addicted—to drugs." Maci stared down at her plate, moving a piece of pancake around in circles. "When I was younger it was mostly booze like my dad, but by the time I was a teenager she'd moved on to harder stuff. The type of drugs you don't get away from without professional help. Not that she's ever wanted help."

His heart ached for Maci already. "That's really hard. I had no idea."

"Studies show that addiction can be genetic." She stared down at her plate. "That was true in my case."

Chance's stomach dropped, but he forced himself not to say anything. He needed to *listen*.

"I started dabbling in middle school. Pot first, then harder stuff as I got older. By the time I was seventeen, I dropped out of school to be my dealer's live-in girlfriend. If I wanted a fix, all I had to do was ask. And do whatever he wanted, of course."

The implications of what she was saying made Chance want to throw up.

She looked up at him. "Whatever you're thinking to put that expression on your face, you're right. I did it all. Prostituted myself for drugs. I'm not the type of person who should be raising a child. Especially not yours."

He frowned. "Especially not mine? What does that mean?"

"It means, look at your life!" She waved her hand around. "You have this great, tight-knit family who would do anything for you. You're the best person I've ever met, and you'll be an even better father. Why do you deserve to be saddled with my baggage forever?"

"Stop." He'd promised his mother he'd listen, but he wasn't going to let Maci tear herself apart like this. "The past only defines us as much as we let it."

She rolled her eyes. "Tell that to a greeting card company, Chance. This is real life. Our choices always come back to haunt us."

"Maybe they do, maybe they don't, but that doesn't matter. You're clean now, right? Been sober for at least as long as I've known you."

There was no way she could've run the office with

such efficiency if she had a drug problem. She was never late, rarely called in sick and was way too sharp to be intoxicated. They would've noticed.

"Yes, I finally got sober a little after my twentieth birthday. My boyfriend got violent one night and I ended up in the hospital. A nurse helped get me into a program and I got clean."

"You got your life together."

She shrugged. "The program helped me. Helped me get clean, helped me get my GED, helped me get some work-training classes under my belt."

For the first time, she'd had a support network, and look at what she'd done once she had it—dragged herself completely out of the pit. "You accepted the help that was offered and changed your life. Everybody would call that admirable."

"Did you not hear the part where I spent years basically selling myself so I could get high? It's amazing I didn't end up dead or with some disease."

He reached over and grabbed her hand. "Yes, I hate to think of you living like that. It absolutely guts me."

"And yet that's what the mother of your child is. A person with addiction who did sex work for drugs."

"The mother of my child is *recovering* from addiction, who survived and got out of a situation that would've destroyed many others. The mother of my child is strong and courageous and capable."

She shook her head, so sadly it broke his heart. "My mother has promised to get sober and fallen off the wagon so many times. What if I'm the same? Addiction runs in my family and I'm passing it along to our daughter. How could you want to be involved with someone like that?"

He had to make her understand something he'd thought about for years. "What about my family and what's passed down?"

Her brows pulled together. "What do you mean?"

"I don't know who either of my biological parents are. There's no info on them. The only thing we know for sure is that they both abandoned me, so they're obviously not the most upstanding of people. Who knows what sort of genetic mess I might be passing down."

"I—"

He put a finger gently over her lips. "Neither of us can stop what we pass down genetically to our children. But both of us can be there to show that any deficiencies we start with don't have to be what defines us. To help them navigate the rough waters."

"I'm afraid I'll be a horrible mom," she whispered.

"There may be patterns from our childhood that both of us have to undo. But, sweetheart, you did so much already with just a little help from the program. Think of all you can do with the full support of all the Pattersons behind you."

She gave him the tiniest smile. "That's a pretty great support network."

For the first time, he had a ray of hope. "You think Tessa or Claire or Kayleigh are going to let you be anything less than the best mother possible? You would do anything for them. They'll do anything for you too."

"I know," she whispered. "I love them. I love your whole family."

"And they love you too. We don't have to tell them all the details, but if you open up to them, you know they'll support you in whatever way they can. I will too."

"Really?"

He pulled her into his arms and rested his forehead against hers. "Yes. And not just because of the baby. You mean the world to me, Maci Ford. We can't change the past and it doesn't matter anyway. I didn't know that Maci, and although I wish I could've helped her, she's gone."

He kissed her gently. "But I know this Maci and she's amazing. All that matters is the future. Our future. Do you understand?"

"No."

He chuckled, pressing his face into her neck so his next words were spoken into her skin. He wanted to imprint them there so she'd never forget. "It means, I'm all in with you, Maci. You and our daughter are my family and I choose the both of you."

He wanted to tell her he loved her, but that could wait. Baby steps.

She sighed and burrowed into his chest. Chance wished he could spend the whole day holding her like this.

"I'm glad you told me everything," he whispered into her hair. "No more running. If you start to feel overwhelmed, we work through it together. Deal?"

"Deal."

Now all he had to do was stop the stalker after her.

Chapter Twenty

Maci was still wrapping her head around the conversation with Chance as they finished eating and did the dishes.

He was still here. Hadn't told her to leave. Hadn't told her he wanted nothing to do with her or the baby. He wasn't acting weird or awkward.

It was more than she could've hoped for. Honestly, more than she could even understand. But he was touching her more, not less. Smiling at her gently in a way she could hardly resist.

And the thing was…she didn't have to resist anymore. He knew all the ugly parts of her past and was still here talking about baby names and something he'd read about pacifiers.

For the first time she had hope for a future that included Chance—which was more than she'd ever let herself dream of.

But a reminder that she had other very real problems came way too soon. Chance's phone chimed and he frowned as he looked down at the message.

"We've got incoming."

"Your parents?" she asked.

"My brothers. They're here."

Chance went and unlocked the door and let them in. All three men looked grim.

"We need to talk," Weston said. Chance nodded.

Luke took a seat at the dining room table. Brax grabbed a cup of coffee and did the same. Weston stood on his side of the table, his body tight with tension. Whatever he was going to tell them, Maci knew it wouldn't be good.

"Should I stay?" she asked.

Luke nodded. "This concerns you most of all."

Chance grabbed her hand and led her to the table, taking the seat next to her.

"First—" Weston rubbed his eyes "—when I got to the office, there was another note from the stalker. Hand delivered this time. It had been slid under the door."

He handed them a note inside a sealed plastic bag. There was also a picture of her and Chance leaving the ob-gyn yesterday.

It looks like congratulations are in order and the ante has been upped. I am up for the battle and will defeat you despite your attempts to stop me.

"He knows about the baby," she whispered. "He was there. He saw us."

"Actually, that image is from the medical complex's security camera," Luke explained. "He probably wasn't there, he just grabbed it later."

That didn't make Maci feel much better. She glanced over at Chance. Fury was burning in his eyes.

Weston held out a hand toward him. "I know you want to lose it right now, but you can't. Believe it or not, it gets worse, and you're going to need to focus."

She could see Chance fight to release the rage enough to focus. Finally, he nodded.

"Even before this delivery this morning, something has been bugging me about the wording of the stalker's notes," Weston continued. "I decided to cast a wide net to see if anything came back. It did. This is—*was*—Brianna Puglisi."

He slid over a printed newspaper article from three years prior in Dallas. Maci frowned as she read about a local hairstylist found dead in her apartment—strangled. She'd barely been twenty-five, but was a favorite of the wealthy ladies in town. More than one of them had lamented over her loss in the article.

"What's this got to do with us?" Chance asked.

"There was a note found with the body. It wasn't published in the paper, of course. I found out about it through some police connections." Weston laid down a printed police report. "I highlighted the relevant part."

Battles require sacrifices. War demands it. I must be the best.

Chance looked up at Weston. "Battle. Wars."

Brax nodded, hands around his coffee mug. "Exactly. Same language as our guy."

Chance muttered a curse. "And he killed her. Not just a stalker."

Weston nodded. "Report states that Brianna had mentioned some weird notes she'd gotten, but she didn't show them to anyone and police didn't find any at her home or work."

"This escalates things," Chance said.

"You have no idea." Luke slid a file across the table. "Once we started looking we found three more. All women in Texas or connecting states. Some stalkings that turned into murders. Some with no proof of stalking, but still a dead woman. But all with the *war, battle, cross fire, be the best* sort of language in notes that were found."

Chance flipped through the police files of the other murders. "So we know there's four dead women."

Brax nodded. "At least. That's what we found in just a few hours this morning by looking for cases with this sort of language involved. There may be more."

Chance didn't look up from the file. "We're dealing with a serial killer."

"A smart one," Weston said. "Killed in different ways so that law enforcement didn't put together what they were dealing with. Even the notes weren't always associated with the killings. Sometimes they were left in a way that made them look like they belonged to the victim."

Maci couldn't stop the whimper that fell from her throat.

Chance pushed the file away and grabbed her hand. He entwined their fingers, stroking his thumb alongside hers in soft, soothing motions, as if he could feel the absolute panic rushing through her.

There was a serial killer on the loose. One who'd announced he was after *her.*

Luke attempted a comforting smile. "As scary as it sounds, it makes sense. We were confused why the stalker was getting violent with little to no provocation when it's not typical for this type of fixation. But if he was a serial killer all along, violence was always the end goal."

She could understand the logic of what he was saying, but it didn't change the fact that a serial killer had set his sights on her.

Chance leaned back in his chair but didn't let go of her hand. "Let's work our way backward. He targeted Maci and us because of our connection to Stella. But I don't recall notes to Stella containing the same war/battle language."

Weston nodded. "You're right. There's nothing in Stella's notes with those words."

"Are we sure we're dealing with the same guy?" Luke asked.

"Definitely the same as those dead women." Brax took the last sip of his coffee, then pushed the mug away. "That language is too specific and similar for it not to be him."

"It's Stella who's the anomaly," Weston said.

Chance's eyes narrowed. "Or…"

He faded off and Maci could almost see his mind spinning, working through various scenarios. Chance was a master at strategy and seeing patterns.

His brothers knew him well enough to give him silence while he worked it out. Maci squeezed his hand, then let it go as he stood up to pace.

"The other victims besides Brianna Puglisi, what did they do for a living?" he asked after a few seconds.

Luke grabbed the file. "Waitress in Houston. Photographer in Albuquerque. Clothing store salesperson in Austin. No evidence that they knew each other at all."

Chance continued pacing. "They didn't have to know each other to be connected. See if they have any connection with Stella."

Weston caught on to his line of thinking first. "We have online access to Stella's calendar. We can look at back dates."

Chance nodded. "Start with the salon Brianna worked at. It catered to the upper echelon. Stella would've been willing to travel to Dallas to get her hair done by the stylist everyone was raving about."

Weston sat down and got out his computer. "Okay, this is going to take a few minutes. Most of Stella's appointments from over a year ago have been archived."

Maci grabbed her phone. There was another, easier way to get this information. It may not have as many details as what Weston would pull up on the calendar, but...

"I've got it," she said. "Stella was at the salon roughly eight months before Brianna was killed."

All four men turned to face her. "How do you know?" Chance asked.

She spun her phone around so they could see. "It

was on her social media. She said she liked Brianna and the style, but didn't know that it would be worth coming to Dallas for every time, so she'd stick with her local stylist in San Antonio."

Maci grabbed the file and flipped to the clothing store salesperson who'd been killed. It was a high-end boutique in Austin. She turned to her phone again and within just a minute had social media proof Stella had been there too.

"Stella has shopped at that clothing boutique in Austin multiple times. No direct proof that she knew the woman who was killed…"

"But the fact that she was there at all ties those two women together." Chance looked around at his brothers. "Stella is the link."

"You think she's the killer?" Maci asked.

Chance shook his head. "No. But somebody close to her probably is."

Weston began typing frantically on his computer.

"But what about all the notes Stella got that aren't the same MO as the war/battle guy?" Brax asked. "Inconsistency doesn't seem to fit for him."

Chance shrugged. "Maybe after the first note he changed his plan or realized his normal language might get him caught. We don't know that he ever planned to harm Stella. Maybe he was just trying to up the ante."

Luke nodded. "This guy wants to be the best. But the best what? Killer? When he talks about winning, what is he referring to?"

With your queen as a prize, I'll do whatever it takes to defeat you.

Maci shuddered as the words he'd written in the note about her came to mind.

Chance rubbed his eyes. "I think we were on the right track when we said this is some sort of professional challenge to him. A matter of pride. He wants to be the best at…whatever it is. Killing, stalking, keeping ahead of law enforcement. Who knows? Stella and her level of security and exposure just upped the challenge for him."

Weston finally looked up from his computer. "I concur and want to take it a step further. I think we were right when we said this guy was former military."

Chance nodded. "We need to check the full security team. Get Dorian in on it. He'd be the best one to say if there's anyone on the team who fits the profile and maybe has been acting strange."

"Before we do that, there's someone else we need to look into. I think your instincts were right all along, Chance." Weston spun the laptop around so everyone could see it. It was a picture of Rich.

"Rich?" Maci asked. "He's not military."

Weston hit a button that brought up a picture of a young Rich in a military uniform. "Nope, but he was Junior ROTC in high school. And his father, who died five years ago, was a decorated marine. Definite military ties we didn't look closely enough into."

"You really think Rich could be a killer?" Maci whispered. She thought of how much time she'd spent with him so close to her and felt sick.

Chance's eyes were already filled with rage. "That smug bastard has been toying with us from the beginning. It damn well is going to end now."

Chapter Twenty-One

Maci went upstairs soon after their discovery, claiming to need a nap, but Chance knew better. She was terrified and he didn't blame her.

If Rich was the stalker—now killer—then she'd been in his grasp more than once. He could have taken her at any time, especially knowing all the security measures in place.

He hadn't done it because it would've made it too obvious they were up against an inside man. Instead he'd bided his time, set the game up for extended play.

Bringing Maci into it as his target had been a mistake. There was no way in hell Chance was going to let anything happen to her.

"We need to figure out a plan of action," he told his brothers.

"We have to be careful who we bring in on this. If Rich is definitely our guy, we don't know what sort of internal measures he has in place to get info."

Chance had no doubt Rich was their guy. "He could have phones tapped. Hell, he could have someone else working with him."

Brax got up to get himself another cup of coffee. "Nobody in the LeBlanc organization would think twice about giving Rich intel. He was handpicked by LeBlanc himself."

Chance rubbed the back of his neck. "The last thing we need is for him to go to ground because he figures out we're on to him." Maci would never be safe.

"I say we go see LeBlanc in person and let him know what we suspect," Luke said. "He needs to make sure Stella is in a safe place where Rich can't get to her."

"Agreed. Then we can check the dates of the murders with Rich's known whereabouts." Chance was ready to move. "Let's get Mom and Dad back here. Someone needs to stay here too, just in case."

Weston pointed at his computer. "I'll stay here and see if there are any more cases I can tie this to. And we're going to have to come up with more than a couple years in ROTC in order for the police to take this seriously. Rich isn't just going to roll over and confess."

Chance nodded. "You're right. Let's make sure everyone is safe, then we'll figure out a further plan. Start pressing your PD contacts. Let's see what we would need for them to make an arrest."

"Once I show all this to my colleagues on the force and they see it's a serial killer, believe me, they'll want to make an arrest. You guys be safe and keep me posted."

Chance ran up to say goodbye to Maci, but she was sleeping. Good, she needed the rest.

He reached over and kissed the top of her head. "I'm

not going to let anyone hurt you." He was talking to both mother and baby.

And he meant every word.

LESS THAN FORTY-FIVE minutes later they were back in LeBlanc's office.

"Gentlemen, should I call in Dorian and his team?" LeBlanc asked. "I'm hoping you actually have something useful for us this time."

The man was frustrated. Chance couldn't blame him.

"We'd actually prefer to speak to you alone, if that's okay," Chance explained. "We've had a breakthrough in the case, and we have reason to believe the stalker may be working inside your organization."

LeBlanc's eyes got wide. "What?"

Chance didn't want the man to panic, so he chose his words carefully. "We've found some similar cases from the past few years that we believe were committed by the same person."

Brax gave the man his most comforting smile. "We have some questions we think will help us nail down who the perp is. But first—do you have confirmation Stella is still safe?"

Once they started making their case against Rich, it was going to tip him off. They needed to have everyone secure before that.

"Yes, I spoke to her not long before you arrived. She's safe, but we're not going to be able to keep her out of the limelight much longer. She's doing a photo shoot at castle ruins in Scotland. That will hold her off a few more days."

Chance glanced over at his brothers. "And Rich? He didn't go over there, did he?"

"No, he stayed here in case he was needed."

"That's good. We might need him. What can you tell us about Rich?"

"He's worked for me for five years. Stella responds well to him so I've kept him around. My one rule was that he wasn't allowed to sleep with her and he's not broken that. Why do you ask?"

Brax shot Chance a look. Chance understood what his brother was communicating: this needed to be handled delicately.

"Before we get into specifics, we need to run a few dates by you and see what you, Stella, Rich, Jason Rogers and your office manager were doing on those days."

LeBlanc was confused. "Marguerite?"

Chance nodded. He'd tossed Jason, one of the main security guards, and Marguerite Frot into the mix for subterfuge. If Rich was listening or had means of accessing what they were talking about, maybe it would throw him off the scent.

LeBlanc sat down at his desk. "Okay, fine. What are the dates? My system will allow us to pull up schedules. It should list what security teams were working also."

Chance wasn't a huge computer person, but he was thankful for this program that was about to make their lives much easier.

Luke read off the dates. They waited as patiently as they could as LeBlanc started with himself and listed what he'd been doing on each day. Then moved to Stella.

Chance grit his teeth when he next listed what Marguerite then Jason had been doing the dates of the murders. Since both of them were red herrings, they didn't matter.

Finally, he got to Rich.

"On the first date, Rich wasn't working. He generally takes Mondays and Tuesdays off since Stella's calendar doesn't tend to be full for those days."

Chance glanced at Luke and Brax. Rich not working meant he'd been free to commit the murder.

"Date two, it looks like Rich had a doctor's appointment. I vaguely remember that. A few weeks later he had a spot taken off on his shoulder that he was concerned might be cancer. Stella was distraught and did a six-week segment on different sunscreens."

"Okay," Chance said. They would have to follow up on that. He may not have gone to the doctor's appointment at all or it could've been very short. It was inconclusive at this point.

"Third date, Rich was not working again."

Chance grabbed his phone, ready to contact Weston. They were three for three with Rich, and Chance was sure LeBlanc was about to say the same for the date of the fourth murder they'd found.

They needed to be ready to move. Brax and Luke had the same tense body language Chance did.

"Okay, date four." LeBlanc clacked on his keyboard. "Oh, I could've given this to you earlier. Rich was with me the whole day that day in Los Angeles."

Chance's brow furrowed. "Are you sure?"

LeBlanc nodded as he looked up from his screen.

"Yes, I remember it now. Half the office and Stella had that stupid virus. Rich was one of the few who tested negative, so he came with me to the opening of a new LeBlanc office branch there. He was acting as part personal assistant, part pretty boy for the press and part security."

Chance spun to face Luke. "What was the time on the fourth case?"

"Midafternoon, Texas time."

Chance looked back at LeBlanc. "You're absolutely sure Rich was with you that whole day? He didn't take a later flight or something?"

"I'm positive. I remember because we were almost late. Flying at that time during the height of the pandemic was problematic, even on a private plane."

Brax handed Chance his phone. Pulled up on it was the press report of the office opening. It had been a bold move on LeBlanc's part, considering most people were working from home, with no indication of returning any time soon.

There was Rich, smiling beside LeBlanc. The footage was time-stamped in a way that meant it was impossible that Rich had killed the fourth woman. When they looked further into the first three, they'd likely find the same thing.

Chance's jaw ached at how hard he was clenching it. Rich was a smug bastard, but he wasn't the killer.

"So, does all this information help you with your theory?" LeBlanc asked.

Brax and Luke looked as frustrated as Chance felt.

"Yes," he finally managed to say. Eliminating suspects was an important step to solving anything. But that didn't make Chance feel any better.

"Then can I ask exactly what this is about? What these *other cases* you're referring to are?"

Luke recovered quickest. "We've come across some disturbing facts, and we need to gather more information before we give you details. For now, let's keep this conversation between us, please."

Chance was trying to wrap his head around the fact that they would have to start back at square one when Dorian entered LeBlanc's office.

"I saw you guys on the door roster. Has there been a breakthrough in the case?"

Nobody answered. Neither Chance nor his brothers wanted to mention the words *serial killer* in front of LeBlanc.

It was LeBlanc who finally took charge. "Evidently, there is some sort of breakthrough but nobody wants to tell me what it is."

Brax tried his charming smile. "Only because we want to make certain of a few things first."

They were about to get fired, Chance could feel it. That was the last thing they needed. Access to information surrounding Stella was going to be critical.

Dorian came to their rescue. "Nicholas, sometimes security teams have to work in ways that don't make sense to the client. You and I had to learn that about each other early on. Let them do the job you hired them for."

"Fine." LeBlanc threw up a hand. "Take them to the

conference room and help them with whatever they need. I have a business to run."

Once they were in the conference room, they explained the situation. They were going to need Dorian's help to catch this bastard.

Dorian sat down hard in one of the plush leather chairs as he took it all in. "Holy hell. We're dealing with a serial killer, not just a stalker?"

They gave him a little time to process it. They'd all felt the same way.

Dorian ran a hand over his jaw. "I need to double Stella's security now. Even though the guy's focus seems to have moved on to someone else."

Maci. Chance would be taking her to ground until this was over. He wasn't taking a chance with her. If he had to move her to a different country too, he'd do it.

"So, what's the killer's motive? How'd you put together that we're dealing with more than a stalker?"

They explained the similarity of terms used in the notes at the murder scenes and the ones the stalker had sent to their office.

"The guy wants a challenge," Dorian said after hearing them out. "Has the need to be the best."

Chance nodded. "That's what we concluded too. We've been looking at people who fit that profile— former military or even law enforcement."

"Agreed." Dorian was studying the reports Luke had brought with him. "I'd also widen the search to look at martial arts or MMA fighters. They use that kind of language also."

"Hell, gamers use it too," Brax muttered. "Maybe we tried to narrow it down too much."

"Honestly, we thought it was Rich," Chance explained. "He had some ROTC experience and his father was military, but it can't be because LeBlanc just provided an alibi for one of the murders."

Everybody grumbled about that.

"And this whole thing with Stella felt like the stalker always had the inside scoop on what we were doing," Chance continued.

"It definitely feels personal. Like he's taunting everyone. And that the choice of victim feels less important than the actual challenge. First Stella, now Maci."

Chance agreed with Dorian's deduction, but the choice of victim was *very* important to him. "This still feels like an inside job to me. Or at least that the stalker/killer is getting inside info from someone."

"We'll run a complete security diagnostic. If there's info being leaked inadvertently from someone on my team, we'll find it."

"And if it's someone leaking it on purpose?" Luke asked.

"We'll find that too. It may take a little longer, but I promise you it will happen."

Chance walked over and shook Dorian's hand. "We're going to keep at it. See if there are any more murders we can link to this. We're bringing in some law enforcement contacts."

Dorian nodded. "That's one of the reasons Nicholas wanted to bring you guys in in the first place—your local contacts and influence here. I'll admit I was skeptical when he first mentioned it. But you've done nothing but prove me wrong."

"Let's just catch this guy," Chance said. "He made it way too personal when he targeted Maci."

Dorian gave him a tight smile. "I completely understand. He's messed with the mother of your unborn child. I'd stomp him into the ground."

"That's exactly what I plan to do."

Chapter Twenty-Two

When Maci woke up from her nap, she wandered down-stairs. Weston was sitting at the kitchen table with his computer. His face was grim. Sheila and Clinton were back. Their faces were grim too.

"Chance, Brax and Luke went to meet with LeBlanc, see if we could get details about Rich. I have law enforcement waiting to move once we do," Weston said once he saw her.

"Okay." She was still having a hard time wrapping her head around the fact that she'd been so close to a possible killer. How many times he'd touched her.

"Do you want something to eat, honey?" Sheila asked.

"No." The word came out as a croak. "Chance made me a really big breakfast."

"Did you two talk?"

Maci nodded. It had only been a few hours ago, but seemed like forever. "Yes. It was good. You were right. Chance could handle my past."

Sheila pulled her in for a hug. "My boy can handle anything. He's going to handle this other thing too. Just you wait."

Maci hoped so. She felt like she couldn't breathe. "I think I might go take a shower, then lay back down."

The older woman smiled gently. "Absolutely. Hopefully you'll be more hungry at dinnertime."

Maci looked back over at Weston. "Did you find anything else?"

His face was almost haggard. "At least one more. I'm still searching."

Five murders.

She couldn't think about it too much right now or she was going to panic. She showered, then got back into bed, pulling the blankets up to her head, trying to shut out the world.

When she awoke the second time, things were actually worse. Her phone was buzzing with a call from her mother.

"What do you want, Evelyn?" Maci kept her voice barely above a whisper so none of the Pattersons would hear her.

"Maci, baby, I'm in trouble."

Maci really didn't have the time or mental energy to deal with her right now. "You're always in trouble."

"Baby." Her mother's voice was small, shaky. "I'm really sorry for how I treated you a couple days ago. That was wrong."

Maci rolled her eyes. "You can't blackmail me for more money. I've already told Chance everything."

"It was wrong for me to say what I did. So wrong. I thought about you being pregnant, and I knew you would need your money for the baby."

"Yes, that's true."

"My dealer has been trying to get me to sell for him for a while, so I told him I would. That way I wouldn't need money from you."

"Timothy?" He was low-level and not organized. Barely more than a thug.

"Yes."

Maci rubbed her eyes. This wasn't what she wanted. "Mom, that's dangerous."

"I know. I—I..." Evelyn let out a sob. "I was robbed last night. They took all the product."

Maci sat up straight in the bed. "Are you hurt?"

"No, but Timothy has given me twenty-four hours to come up with the money or he will hurt me. You know, he has to set an example." She listed the amount she needed.

"Mom, I don't have that much! Especially not since you just cleaned me out."

"I know. I know." Evelyn began to cry in earnest. "I don't know what to do. And it gets worse."

Oh, no. "What did you do?"

"Timothy was threatening to break my wrist when I told him I didn't think I could get the money. So I mentioned where you work." Her voice got smaller. "I think he's planning to jump your boyfriend or his brothers to get the money if I don't pay him back."

Maci thought through finances. If she pooled everything from every account and maxed out the cash withdrawal on her one credit card, then she might just have enough.

At least enough to keep Timothy and his buddies from attacking the Pattersons unawares while they were in the middle of a crisis. Maci could handle this for them. They would never even need to know.

And she could admit that, even though Chance already knew about her past, she'd prefer not to dump this on him in life-size Technicolor.

"Where are you, Mom?"

Her mom spit out an address on the south side of town near the warehouse district. Not the safest place, but not where Rich Carlisle would be hanging out, so at least she didn't have to worry about a serial killer.

Just run-of-the-mill family drug drama. No problem.

She disconnected the call and got dressed. There was no way Weston was going to let her go handle this, so she wasn't going to tell him. He had more important things to do. So did Chance.

She left a brief note on the pillow explaining she was going to see her mother in case someone wandered up to check on her. She didn't want them to think she'd been kidnapped.

She could hear Weston talking to his parents in the kitchen as she crept downstairs and out the back door. Luke had brought her car over a couple nights ago and left it parked on the street, so she slipped around the house and inside it.

She winced as the car started, hoping Weston wouldn't hear. Chance would kill her if he found out what she was doing. She pulled away from the curb.

So, she'd make sure he wouldn't find out.

"Weston has found one more murder tied to this guy and is checking further into another," Luke said as they walked back into the San Antonio Security office. "He's shown everything to his PD contacts, so it's more than just us looking into it now."

"Good. We need as many eyes on this as possible." Chance didn't care who figured out the identity of the killer. He just wanted Maci safe. "I'm going to take Maci out of town. Get us into a safe house nobody knows about. Mom and Dad's place is too easily connected to us."

Weston had been providing all clear updates since they'd left, but Chance didn't want to leave Maci there any longer than necessary.

"Agreed," Brax said. "Maybe we can get Stella to impersonate Maci to catch this guy."

Chance managed a grim smile at his brother's joke.

"You decide on a place to hide out with Maci. I'm going to start looking harder at the ob-gyn angle. How did he know you guys were going there?"

Brax froze. "We were talking about it here at the office before you went."

Luke and Chance froze too. If the killer had heard their plans, that meant he was either using a parabolic mic or had planted a bug in the office.

His brothers had realized the same thing. They all started searching for hidden recording devices in the office.

They found three.

Chance tilted his head toward the back door, and they went out into the alley so they could talk without being heard.

"Planted bugs means the person was in our office,"

Chance said. "He would know about Mom and Dad's house. I've got to get Maci out of there right away."

"Okay, we'll look into moving the office to a secondary location until we can make sure it's clean," Luke said.

"Good news is, this narrows down our pool of suspects quite a bit," Brax said. "There's only been a half a dozen of Dorian's team members here over the past few weeks. It's got to be one of them. I'll call him."

Chance was about to nod when Dorian's parting words when they left LeBlanc's building came back to him.

He's messed with the mother of your unborn child.

The curse that fell from Chance's mouth was vile. Both brothers turned to stare at him.

"Did you guys tell anybody at LeBlanc's office that Maci is pregnant?" he asked.

"Hell no," Luke said. "We didn't even tell Mom and Dad."

"It's Dorian," Chance whispered. "He's the killer. He knew Maci was pregnant today when he shouldn't have."

All three men sprinted back inside to cut to the front door and get to their vehicles. Chance had his phone in his hand and was dialing Nicholas LeBlanc.

"Patterson," LeBlanc answered. "Unless you have some sort of—"

"Lock down your building," Chance cut him off. "Do it right now."

Locking down the building would keep Dorian trapped inside.

"What? Why would—"

"Do it!" Chance yelled.

He heard LeBlanc initiate the lockdown.

"Okay, it's done. In fifteen seconds no one will be able to get in or out."

"It's Dorian Cane. He's the stalker. He's not only a stalker, he's a killer—that's what we found out with the other cases."

"That's impossible." LeBlanc's tone was heavy with shock.

"I'll prove it later. Right now, keep your office door locked until the police get there. Don't let Dorian in there with you for any reason." The last thing they needed was a hostage situation.

He could hear LeBlanc clicking at his keyboard. "I don't have to worry about that. Dorian left just a couple of minutes after you did."

Chapter Twenty-Three

It was depressing how little time it took Maci to liqui-
date nearly every cent she had available to her name.
Twenty minutes after leaving Clinton and Sheila's
house, she had the cash in hand and was on her way
to meet Evelyn.

She parked outside the warehouse address, surprised
her mother wasn't there to snatch the money out of
Maci's hand like she'd done in the past.

Maci got out of the car and began walking toward
the warehouse. This was it. This was the last time she
was helping Evelyn in this way. The only thing Maci
would be willing to help pay for from now on would
be some sort of rehab.

"Evelyn?" Maci didn't know where her mom was,
but she needed to get back to the Pattersons' house before they discovered she was gone. "Come on, Mom. I
don't have time for this."

She called Evelyn's phone but got no answer. She got
all the way to the warehouse before deciding to turn
back. There was no way she was going into an aban-

doned warehouse by herself, and for whatever reason Evelyn wasn't here.

She turned and shrieked when she found a man behind her. Fortunately, she recognized him quickly.

"Dorian Cane, right? Oh, my gosh, you scared me."

He smiled. "Sorry, wasn't my intent."

"Oh, no. Did Chance send you to get me?" Damn it, had he already figured out she was gone? She was in so much trouble.

"Um, yes. Chance sent me. Wanted me to escort you somewhere safe. Things have escalated."

She nodded. "Rich, right? Ends up he's a killer, not just a stalker."

"Yes, Rich. Fooled us all. Chance really didn't want you out here alone and… I was close by, so I offered to come get you."

"I was supposed to meet my mother. You haven't seen an older lady around, have you?"

"No, I haven't. We should go."

"Yeah, I'm sure Chance wants to yell at me as soon as possible too."

Dorian smiled. "Only because he cares. I understand that."

They began walking back toward the cars.

"Yeah, you two are probably cut from the same cloth. It's what makes you good at your jobs."

"Yes, this job is a battle. Getting to know Chance and the other Patterson brothers has certainly made me a better me. I've always strived to be the best."

Maci tensed at his words. They were way too similar to the notes that had been left. She stopped.

"You know what? I should probably make one more sweep to be certain my mom's not here. Do you mind waiting just a second?"

There was no way she was getting into a vehicle with Dorian until she talked to Chance. Maybe she was being paranoid, but under the circumstances, that could be forgiven.

She forced a smile at Dorian. "Just hang out here for two minutes. I'll be right back." She turned back toward the warehouse. "Mom? You here?"

She walked, calling for Evelyn as she pulled her phone out. She was just hitting Chance's number when a soft voice spoke behind her.

"You're not a pale imitation at all, are you?"

Maci tried to breathe through the terror. This was the voice from that night at the apartment when she'd been knocked unconscious.

Dorian was definitely the killer.

She turned to face him again. "You. Why?"

"Someone has to be the best. Learning how to stalk, learning how to kill… It made me the best security expert available."

"But you're Stella's stalker. How can you be the best at protecting someone when you're the one putting her in danger?"

"I never planned to hurt Stella—she's not worth the time or effort. I wasn't even her real stalker at first. I eliminated him early on and took over. Especially once Nicholas brought in the Pattersons. I quickly realized how much I could learn by going up against them. And knew I could up the ante when I targeted someone they cared so much about… *You*."

Maci took a few steps backward, trying to figure out what to say. "I'm just their employee."

He tsked and shook his head. "You're the mother of Chance Patterson's child. He would burn the world to the ground to get you back. His brothers would hold the matches for him."

"I'm not going with you."

Dorian smiled and slowly pulled up his pants leg at the calf, showing some sort of knife holder. "I don't think you're going to have a choice."

Without another word, Maci spun and ran. She didn't make it far before Dorian's arms wrapped around her from behind, stopping her progress. At least he didn't have the knife out yet.

She remembered what Chance had taught her in their training. She used her legs to kick back, aiming for his knees, groin, whatever. Dorian let out a curse as her foot connected to a sensitive spot and let her go.

She dropped her phone in the skirmish but didn't stop to pick it up. She sprinted as hard as she could for the warehouse.

She knew if Dorian got her into his car, she and her baby would be his next victims.

"WHAT DO YOU mean she's not there?"

Chance was ready to put his fist through a wall. He'd called Maci's phone half a dozen times, and each time it had gone directly to voice mail.

"We all thought she was taking a nap," Weston said.

"She left a note on the pillow saying she needed to meet her mom and would be right back."

He'd already explained that Dorian was a killer and law enforcement had an APB out for his arrest.

That wouldn't help if he already had Maci.

The door to the office opened and Chance turned to bark that they were closed. "I'll call you back," he said to Weston when he saw who it was.

Evelyn Ford. And she had seen better days.

He rushed to her and helped her sit down. She had blood seeping from a head wound. "Mrs. Ford, where's Maci? What happened?"

His brothers rushed in to see what was going on, but remained silent.

"I needed money. She was supposed to meet me about a half hour ago."

"She didn't show up?"

"I don't know. Some man saw me, said he worked with you. Offered to give me the money I needed to pay back my dealer."

Chance grabbed a file and showed her a picture of Dorian. "This man?"

"Yes, that's him. I thought I was doing Maci a favor, not taking her money. You know, so she could save it for the baby. But then the guy knocked me on the head and dragged me into an alley."

"Evelyn, where's Maci? Her phone is offline, so we can't track it. I've got to find her."

"Guy left me with the money. I paid someone a hundred of it to get me here. I needed to tell you that my dealer may be coming after you."

He didn't understand what she was talking about and didn't have time to get her to explain.

"Evelyn, listen to me. My brothers and I can handle any drug dealer. We'll get you someplace safe so he can't hurt you either. But if you know where Maci is, you need to tell me right now."

Every second they wasted gave Dorian more time to hurt Maci.

"I was supposed to meet her at the warehouse district. I needed the money to pay back Timothy, my dealer. I promise I didn't mean any of those things I said to Maci." Evelyn started to cry.

He and Maci were going to have a talk—*again*—about the things she was keeping from him. But he needed to find her first.

"Where, Evelyn? Focus."

She got out the address.

"I'll stay with her and make sure no drug dealers do whatever she was talking about," Brax said. "I'll get PD there immediately too."

"Give us five minutes. Sirens may spook him into hurting her."

Brax nodded and Chance sprinted for his car, Luke on his heels.

MOST OF THE warehouses in this section of town had been abandoned years ago after a storm had caused massive flood damage. Maci could scream, but there probably wouldn't be anyone around to hear her.

And screaming at this point would tell Dorian exactly where she was.

She found an open door and rushed into a building. Hiding was her best option. It was dark in here, the only light from an emergency exit sign near another door at the side.

She ran for the far corner, zigzagging around various piles of crates and abandoned machinery. The door behind her opened and closed, and there was silence.

Maci struggled to hear anything over the pounding of her own heart.

The most important thing is to keep your head. Use your strengths.

She could hear Chance's voice in her mind. He was right. If she panicked, this was over.

"Now, now, Maci," Dorian taunted. "I love a good game of hide-and-seek, but this isn't your style, is it? You're more of a confronting things head-on type of gal, aren't you?"

She wasn't about to answer and give away her position. She needed to make her way around to the other door and try to get out.

He flipped on a phone flashlight, and she jerked her head back behind the crate she hid behind. The light would give Dorian more of an advantage.

"Do you understand the need to be the best at something, Maci? I was the best in my platoon until a stray bullet ended that part of my life. Do you know what it is to have the thing that is most important to you snatched away?"

Like a murderer trying to end you and your unborn child's lives? Yeah, I do, asswipe.

How she longed to say the words out loud.

"Then I had to find a new career pathway on which to be the best. Private security fit the bill."

He got quiet after that and the light switched off. She crept farther away from where she'd last heard his voice, keeping her body low and small.

"I've killed nine women."

Maci struggled to keep her surprised gasp silent. He was trying to get a reaction from her—any indication of her location.

"But listen, Maci, before you think bad of me... I did it for a purpose. Do you understand? With every woman I killed I became better at personal security. I learned more about how killers thought and what could be done to protect someone from a killer. Those women's deaths had *meaning*."

He was a complete psychopath. Could see no wrong in what he'd done.

The flashlight switched back on, aimed for where she'd been just a few moments ago. Damn it, he was expecting her to stay low to the ground. She needed to get higher, climb on some of the machinery all over this place. Dorian hadn't shone any light up there at all.

You're smart. A quick thinker. Use that to your advantage.

She found some debris on the ground—a piece of metal that had broken off something—and grabbed it. She threw it with all her might in the opposite direction of where she planned to go.

Then she scurried up onto what seemed to be some sort of bottling equipment piece, careful not to make any noise. That allowed her to move onto a conveyer belt a few feet higher that held her weight easily.

Dorian's light switched off once again when he heard the noise. When it came back on, it wasn't pointed in the direction she'd hoped. It was right where she'd been five seconds ago.

If he pointed his light up now, she would be caught.

She swallowed her whimper.

The light switched off again. "Your death will have meaning too, Maci. So will the Patterson brothers'. I can't leave them alive. Leaving your enemy alive means you always have to be looking over your shoulder."

She held still. He was waiting for her to make a mistake. The slightest one and she'd be dead.

"Your mother too, probably, if she doesn't take care of that herself. She's got a pretty severe drug habit, you know. Was more than happy to take the money I gave her, although was probably less happy when I knocked her unconscious. I traced her phone. That's how I found you."

Maci had to push thoughts of her mother aside. She had to push everything aside but this moment.

Survival is always the most important thing.

She was going to survive. She had too much to live for not to.

The light came back on, once again looking in hidden corners and in low places to hide. It wouldn't take much longer for him to figure out she wasn't down there.

But in the silence, she heard the most beautiful sound: sirens.

The light switched off again. "Looks like the game has changed, Maci, and we won't be able to finish today. What a shame. But don't worry, I'll be back for you. For all of you. I'm the best, so you can count on that."

In that moment Maci knew she couldn't let Dorian leave. He was telling the truth: he would be back. And one by one the people she loved would fall to his madness. Including her daughter. Maci had no doubt Dorian would hunt her too, even if it took years.

Maci could stop this right now. She *had* to stop it right now. Even if it cost her everything.

She stretched out her hand and found a small metal pipe. It wouldn't be much against that knife he'd taunted her with earlier, but she just needed to stop him long enough for the police to get here. The sirens were getting louder.

She shut everything out and listened for Dorian. As he passed under her she grit her teeth and let herself fall off the side of the conveyor belt on top of him.

Light flashed inside the warehouse from the far door as she fell, but she ignored it. She would only get one chance at this.

She landed hard on Dorian, swinging her pipe and yelling as loud as she could to let the police know where they were. She got two hits in before a blow to her face threw her backward.

She tried to get back to her feet but he was already over her, knife in hand. He grabbed the pipe out of her hand and threw it to the side, then pulled her up by her shirt.

"I am the best," he said simply.

He slashed the knife toward her chest, and she knew this was the end. She closed her eyes, waiting for the pain, distraught that she'd failed. Devastated she'd never told Chance she loved him.

But the pain never came.

She heard multiple cracks of thunder over the roaring around her but didn't open her eyes.

"Maci! Maci, open your eyes, baby. Come on."

Chance? She could barely hear him.

"Stop screaming, sweetheart. It's okay. I've got you. Dorian is dead."

All that noise was coming from *her*. She hadn't even realized it. She closed her mouth and silence surrounded them.

"Are you okay? Did he hurt you?" Chance was frantically pressing his hands all over her body, searching for wounds.

Luke was standing over Dorian, weapon raised. Dorian wasn't moving.

"I'm okay," she managed to get out. "I'm okay. I had to stop him. He was going to hurt you. Hurt everyone. I couldn't let him—"

Chance's lips pressed hard against hers and he pulled her against his chest.

"You did it. Dorian Cane will never hurt anybody ever again."

Chapter Twenty-Four

Three weeks later

"No, don't you dare touch me, Chance Patterson! If we are late to family dinner everyone will know what we've been doing."

Chance grinned from where he was stalking Maci in the kitchen of his house, loving the way she laughed as she threw her arms out in front of herself to keep him away.

As if she could keep him away.

As if anything was ever going to keep him away from her again.

He grabbed one wrist and used it to yank her closer. "We both took a full week off work and locked ourselves in this house without talking to anyone. I'm pretty sure everyone knows what we've been doing."

But they'd needed it. They'd needed a chance to decompress after what had happened with Dorian. Needed a chance to rest and be with each other.

Chance had definitely needed the opportunity to

hold Maci close to him and reassure himself that she and the baby were really okay.

That could've so easily not have been the case.

Getting to Maci at that warehouse had been the longest twenty minutes of his life. Kicking open that door and watching her drop down onto a serial killer? Watching Dorian lift that knife to end her life?

Even knowing he and Luke had each plugged three bullets into Dorian, he would have nightmares about the image until the day he died.

Nicholas and Stella LeBlanc had been traumatized too by the thought that someone they'd trusted had been so evil. Stella had then figured out how to use it to become even more popular on social media.

Maci pressed her lips against his. "We can't be late. Mom is going to be there."

It was a first step for Evelyn, one they were delighted she was taking. She was a long way from kicking her drug habit, but joining them for dinner was at least a step in the right direction. Hopefully they would be able to show her some rehab options and she'd agree to treatment.

Maci had made it clear to Evelyn that if she wanted to be a part of the baby's life, she was going to need to be clean. They would help her as much as they could, but ultimately the choice had to be Evelyn's.

He kissed Maci tenderly. He'd kissed her so often over the past few weeks that they both should've been tired of it by now, but neither of them could get enough.

"I love you," she whispered. He would never get tired of hearing her say it.

"I love you too." And he would never get tired of saying it back.

He planned to do it every day for the rest of their lives.

Epilogue

One year later

Sheila Patterson's favorite place to be had always been the kitchen. As a child, it had been the heart of her parents' home, and she'd been determined to make it the heart of her own as well.

Though their usual Sunday dinner was still hours away, the house was already overrun with family.

Weston and Kayleigh had arrived first, their arms loaded down with drinks and snack packs for the kids. Instead of offering to cook, which wasn't always her strong suit, Kayleigh had kept Sheila company, talking all about her newest photography series and how Weston had transformed yet another elderly neighbor's garden into a little piece of paradise.

Sheila listened as Kayleigh spoke about her husband with pride, peeking up from food prep occasionally to see her son glancing at his wife, their eyes equally full of love and devotion. It soothed something in her to see her quietest child find the love of his life.

Halfway through an anecdote that involved a rampaging Weston and a mole he couldn't catch, Brax, Tessa and Walker arrived. The moment Walker saw his favorite auntie, Kayleigh's attention had been stolen, but Sheila didn't mind. She'd sat Tessa on a stool in the kitchen and talked baby names while sneaking her treats before dinner.

Tessa and Brax were pregnant with another boy, and the way Brax looked at her…it was like no one else existed when she was in the room. Like she was the light his life had always needed. And Walker? He was overjoyed at the idea of a baby brother to play with.

Luke and Claire's arrival was followed by much shrieking from Walker once he saw they'd brought their Maine coon cat, Kahn. Claire, once shy and quiet around them all, immediately began telling a story of a second cat they were adopting. Luke kept a firm arm around her waist, his eyes brimming with love too.

Sheila was putting the final touches on everyone's favorite potpie when the sound of cheers told her the last of her family had arrived. First through the door, Maci was glowing, even though little Autumn was five months old and had barely slept since she'd arrived earth side.

Still, there was a calmness that motherhood—and Chance—had brought Sheila's final daughter-in-law. A peace that had allowed her to settle into the family and really open herself up to the rest of the Patterson clan.

Evelyn had joined too. It hadn't been an easy road, and there had been more than one setback, but the woman was trying. For her daughter, for her granddaughter.

But most importantly, for herself.

Sheila looked around the chaos and couldn't help but smile. Her family was here, made up of every skin tone and bound together by love.

Clinton wrapped his arm around her waist and pressed a kiss to her neck. "Remember how distraught we were when they told us we would never have children? Did you ever imagine we'd have this?"

Sheila took a look around at the sounds of yelling and laughter, the mess of toys already spilling out from the living room, the crush of bodies crowded into the kitchen.

Not only did she have four sons, but she'd gained four daughters.

She had a family that was happy, healthy and so full of love you could see it the second you walked into the room.

"No," she told Clinton, burrowing farther into the comfort of his embrace. "I would've never imagined this. But the reality is so much better."

* * * * *

In case you missed the previous books in USA TODAY *bestselling author Janie Crouch's miniseries, San Antonio Security, look for:*

Texas Bodyguard: Luke
Texas Bodyguard: Brax
Texas Bodyguard: Weston

You'll find them wherever Harlequin Intrigue books are sold!

#2169 MARKED FOR REVENGE
Silver Creek Lawmen: Second Generation • by Delores Fossen
Five months pregnant, Deputy Ava Lawson faces her most unsettling murder case yet—the victims are all found wearing a mask of *her* face. Her ex, Texas Ranger Harley Ryland, will risk everything to protect Ava from the killer out for revenge.

#2170 TEXAS SCANDAL
The Cowboys of Cider Creek • by Barb Han
Socialite Melody Cantor didn't murder the half brother she never knew—and former rodeo star Tiernan Hayes is hell-bent on proving it. But when their investigation exposes dangerous family secrets, will Melody be proven innocent...or collateral damage?

#2171 PURSUIT AT PANTHER POINT
Eagle Mountain: Critical Response • by Cindi Myers
Years ago, tragedy brought sheriff's deputy Lucas Malone and shop owner Anna Trent together. When a missing person case reunites them, they'll battle an unknown drug smuggler—and their developing romantic feelings—to uncover the deadly truth.

#2172 WYOMING MOUNTAIN COLD CASE
Cowboy State Lawmen • by Juno Rushdan
Sheriff Daniel Clark and chief of police Willa Nelson must work together to find a murderer. But when Willa suspects her brother, a former cult member, could be involved, her secrets threaten not only their investigation, but the tender bond the two cops have formed.

#2173 SPECIAL AGENT WITNESS
The Lynleys of Law Enforcement • by R. Barri Flowers
When Homeland Security agent Rosamund Santiago witnesses her partner's execution, federal witness protection is her only hope. Falling for small-town detective Russell Lynley only complicates things. And with a criminal kingpin determined to silence the prosecution's only witness, danger isn't far behind...

#2174 RESOLUTE INVESTIGATION
The Protectors of Boone County, Texas • by Leslie Marshman
Struggling single mom Rachel Miller may have wanted to throttle her deadbeat ex-husband, but kill him? Never. Chief Deputy Adam Reed vows to prove her innocence. But his investigation shifts into bodyguard detail when Rachel becomes the killer's next target.

YOU CAN FIND MORE INFORMATION ON UPCOMING HARLEQUIN TITLES, FREE EXCERPTS AND MORE AT HARLEQUIN.COM.

HICNM0823

HARLEQUIN
PLUS

Try the best multimedia subscription service for romance readers like you!

Read, Watch and Play.

Experience the easiest way to get the romance content you crave.

Start your **FREE TRIAL** at
<u>www.harlequinplus.com/freetrial</u>.